Wielding Magic

A Court of Wizards Story

Wielding Magic

A Court of Wizards Story

Kummam Al Maadeed

Hamad Bin Khalifa University Press
P O Box 5825
Doha, Qatar

www.hbkupress.com

Chapter header illustrations by Khadija Mo.

All rights reserved.

No part of this publication may be reproduced or transmitted in any form or by any means, electronic or mechanical, including photocopying, recording, or any information storage or retrieval system, without prior permission in writing from the publishers.

No responsibility for loss caused to any individual or organization acting on or refraining from action as a result of the material in this publication can be accepted by HBKU Press or the author.

First English edition in 2023

ISBN: 9789927161803

Printed in Beirut-Lebanon

Qatar National Library Cataloging-in-Publication (CIP)

Al-Maadeed, Kummam, author.

Wielding magic : a count of wizards story / Kummam Al-Maadeed. First English edition. – Doha, Qatar : Hamad Bin Khalifa University Press, 2023.

208 pages ; 20 cm

ISBN 978-992-716-180-3

1. Magic -- Juvenile fiction. 2. Witches -- Juvenile fiction. 3. Children's stories, English. I. Title.

PZ8. M33 2023
823.92 – dc 23   20232861785x

To Abeer
For wanting this story to be "more"

CHAPTER 1

I am Tia, Wielder of Stars and Protector of Paiza. I can do this.

I tried to settle my nerves as I directed my powers into a pipe made of see-through glass that was set on a table in front of me. It was filled with raw gray steam and I only had one job; to fuse my magic with it and turn it into the shimmering clear steam everyone wanted.

"Steady, child," Burk whispered from across the table.

I closed my eyes and let my magic seep through the glass. I bit my lips as I felt the steam's particles dance around my magic. I pushed further. *Come on, melt together.* But the particles stayed apart. They were grazing my magic, teasing me and floating away the more I pushed.

Come on!

"Steady," Burk whispered again.

I pulled back, then with an irritated huff I pushed with everything I had. The steam expanded and all I heard was a loud bang as I was thrown onto my back. The whole room became engulfed in black smoke.

"Oh, dear," I heard Burk say, as I sat up.

He waved his hand, calling a spell. The cloud of smoke floated out of a small window behind him. I rubbed my cheeks and traces of soot were left all over my fingers.

"Bubbles! I give up," I said standing up. This was the fifth pipe that exploded in my face, today.

"I have to admit, I knew that wielders' magic couldn't replicate the Steam Fusion spell," Burk said, dusting off his robes, "but since your powers are that powerful, I had hoped you could do it."

"If the ancient spell is working just fine, why do you need to replicate it?" I said, as I grimaced at the sight of my fuzzed up curls.

"If we can replicate it, we can give the secret to the cities and kingdoms around us to prevent any future attacks," Burk explained with a frown as he called upon all the glass shards and discarded valves to float into a big bin.

"But if they knew the secret, everyone would produce the clear better steam and Paiza won't have all this wealth."

"Sharing the wealth does not mean losing it."

"Not everyone likes to share," I sighed, slumping into a metal chair. I took a deep breath and let my eyes wonder around the small square room Burk and I had been working in for the past three hours, trying to figure out if wielders' magic could reveal the steam's ancient secret. The room was gray and mostly empty except for a table, a couple of metal chairs and few dusty stacks of paper left in the corner. It wasn't special, but its location was. It was located inside a factory, where most of the steam transformation business occurred. Before coming here, Burk and I had unsuccessfully spent days trying the spell in our workshop back at the castle, without much success, so Burk thought perhaps being in the factory would inspire me.

Obviously, it didn't.

"Why can't we try this at the clock tower again?" I said. It was the location where the fusing magic was happening.

"The magic there is too powerful, we can't perform any spell without it interfering or clashing with your powers," Burk said as he pulled up a new pipe filled with steam onto the table, before adding in his usual cheerful tone, "cheer up, child. We can't expect to figure out the secrets of a thousand year-old spell in mere few attempts."

"A spell that you guessed. No-one even knows the actual spell! Not even the high members of the Court of Wizards!" I said, frustratedly, as I banged my head on the table in protest.

Burk winced, not at my outrage, but at the mention of the high members, who we only talked about once after I'd revealed that I, too, was a high member. You see, all magic across the kingdoms are controlled by a group of very powerful wielders who reside at the Court of Wizards. I grew up there, but it was a horrid place. After I was named a high member, following the discovery that I was a very powerful wielder, they forced me to abuse my powers. I fled there last spring to come work as an assistant to Paiza's only magician, Burk, because Paiza was the only city across the land not under the rule of the Court of Wizards.

"And if they knew the spell..." I trailed off, not wanting to say *they would take Paiza*. It was a place I grew to love, the place I now called home.

"Look at me child," Burk said, squinting his eyes in a very stern way. I did as he asked. "What do we say when we think dark thoughts?"

I took a deep breath, recalling every word.

"They have no claim on me," I said, reciting each word individually with determination, hoping that one day I would believe them.

"No, they do not," Burk said before returning to setting up the pipes again.

Bubbles. He was right. I've always said I ran away from court, but in honesty being a high member was just a job that anyone could quit from. Yet, the thing was, nobody ever did. The place was like a prison with all the laws and the way they controlled my every move. I hated it there, so I *left*. Yet, according to Burk, they didn't come looking for me. There was no news of any missing high members, in any magical correspondence.

Perhaps they gave up on me? Or perhaps they were waiting for me to show myself? Sadly, I did show myself a few months ago when Paiza was attacked by a neighboring city, and I had to reveal my true powers to literally everybody. It was quite the theatrical fight. Burk was super proud. It was also a loud fight, loud enough for the court to hear about it.

My head throbbed and my shoulders tensed.

"I don't want to try the spell again," I whined. He frowned in a sad way. "I can't, Burk, like for bubble's sake. I can't."

"How about a tour of the factory then?" said a voice from behind me that sent my whole surroundings bursting into bright colors.

I turned and smiled at the sight of Rhein, my favorite inventor and the King of Paiza, in all of his black outfit glory, standing at the door.

"Hey. I thought you were working all day today," I said standing and waiting to be hugged, because after failing all morning, I needed a hug.

His face was lit up by his croaked smile that broke the harshness of his scar, as he opened his arms to embrace me.

His blanketing arms were immediately around me and the warmth and strength of his body pushed all my frustration away and filled me with coziness and comfort.

"Chi had to attend to a matter in the farm, so our meeting was postponed," he said, breaking the hug.

Then out of nowhere I felt something shoved on my head, gently, but suddenly.

"Bubbles, what is that?"

"A helmet," Rhein said with a smirk as he tightened a strap under my chin, "for your safety."

I reached up to touch it. It was made of leather and covered my whole head, leaving only my face and few purple curls. "I probably look like an upside mushroom."

"A very cute mushroom," he said, cheekily. I giggled and his hands tightened their grip on my waist, which sent flutters of butterflies across my body. He leaned in, kissing the star tattoo under my eyes before Burk, spoiler of joy, coughed.

"Hello, Burk," Rhein said, his eyes still on me.

"Greetings, your Majesty," Burk replied in a very official tone.

"May I borrow Tia for the rest of the day?" Rhein asked, as if him taking me wasn't already decided.

"Of course, your Majesty, of course. We can work on the spell tomorrow," Burk said with a dramatic bow.

Rhein took my hand and we left. I then realized that when I came this morning, I was perhaps too anxious or too sleepy to register the beauty of the place, or perhaps it was the new prospect of spending the rest of the day with Rhein, but the factory was spectacular.

The whole place was one big hall with a high ceiling and huge windows that were covered in spots of soot and steam residue that allowed just enough sun to sneak through and glow up all the copper and iron metal inside. It was like one huge greenhouse for inventions. We stood before a metallic moving belt that cut the hall into two parts. One was clean and had some metal chairs along the belt, which were occupied with inventors wearing their goggles and leather helmets. Each one had a specific role along the belt. Some screwed valves into containers, tested their pressure and others just moved rods and pushed buttons, which I assumed was very important work. On the other side and closer to the windows, a cluster of tables with tall piles of papers and tiny sharp gadgets were located along with a group of very chatty inventors.

In between the organized chaos, three pillars shot up to the ceiling with open spiral staircases, that led to a circular balcony that floated above us like trees. The place was a metallic forest.

"This way," Rhein said, as we walked between the busy inventors, who didn't flinch at the sight of the King walking among them. They were used to him. His visits had increased over the past couple of months, as work on new inventions to enhance Paiza's security and production of steam increased.

As we walked across the belt, the machine's noises grew louder and when we reached the other side of the hall, Rhein stopped. Before us and across the whole wall, was one big flat machine. Glass shields protected dials, tiny valves and metal wheels that were scattered across it, whilst the huge pipes that emerged from it, were installed into the belt.

Three inventors hung onto the machine via thin ropes that descended from the ceiling and were tied around their waists. They flew gracefully from one square to the next, checking the numbers and turning a wheel or two.

"The control panel!" Rhein shouted over all the noise. He was proud of that panel; I could see it in his eyes. Something about those inventions brought pure passion onto his normally stern royal face.

Bubbles! It was taking everything in me not to reach up and kiss his jaw in front of every inventor in that factory. I focused on the control panel and was about to ask Rhein something, when someone screamed.

I looked up and saw that one of the ropes had snapped, dropping one inventor from a dangerous height.

"Hex!" I cursed, raising my left hand. I intended for my power to save him, but a deep sharp sting cut through my forearm. I bit my lips, but the inventor was about to hit the hard ground. There was no time for me to react to this weird pain. My right hand immediately moved, and a thread of light shot from my fingers and wrapped around his body, stopping him an inch from the ground. His nose barely grazing the ground.

The pain in my forearm vanished completely. I blinked and flexed my wrists. I was feeling totally fine. It was as if I'd imagined the whole thing. Perhaps I did?

Rhein ran toward the inventor and helped him to his feet.

"Are you alright?"

The inventor, who was just a young boy with ruffled red hair and freckles was shaken, but nodded. His hand reached for the three rusty goggles that hung from his neck. They were really old and in three different sizes. He mouthed, *one, two, three,* as his fingers touched each. He was calming himself.

One of the two other inventors flew down toward us and hugged the boy. This inventor was a middle-aged woman and had the same ruffled red hair. *His mom?*

"Thank you," she shouted before taking him away.

I turned to ask Rhein if that was the young boy's mom, when I saw darkness fall upon his face. All the proud passion disappeared, leaving nothing, but a cold royal face. I reached out, hoping to touch his arm, but he dismissed me and walked out.

Hexing cauldrons.

I ran behind him between pipes, buffs of steam and rushing inventors, because, bubbles, he was so fast. He didn't stop until he found a door, pushed against it and stepped outside.

I blinked at the bright light of the noon sun and realized we were standing in a narrow alley. The factory was located close to the market circle behind the clock tower, so we could hear the busy noises of the sellers and buyers, but no-one was passing this side of city.

It would've been nice to be here and feel the fresh air and inhale the smell of moss and flowers after being cooped up in the factory all morning, but I was worried about Rhein, who had started pacing in a short line, going back and forth.

"I need to talk to Chi. We need better ropes. Better materials," he said.

His eyes were focused on the stone ground and his hand pushed back his new short hair. He always did that when he was worried or thinking really hard. He was obviously doing both.

"It was an accident, and nothing happened," I said, trying to calm him, but I realized it was the wrong thing to say as he stopped pacing and his frown deepened.

"An accident is a result of recklessness. One wrong move and the consequences are dire," he said so softly, it ached my heart. I shouldn't have said that word. It always brought back the memory of an accident he had many years ago. The accident that gave him two sharp scars that ran from his jaw down to his chest and the accident in which a colleague inventor of his had died.

"I know," I took his hand. "Come sit with me."

We sat on the step of the door. He closed his eyes and squeezed my hand. I leaned in and rested my head on his arm. We sat there in silence.

I don't know how being with Rhein had become so normal and easy. Ever since I had slept for three days straight, following the battle of the wall, Rhein and I had been getting closer each day. Trying to spend every free moment together whenever we could find one. I couldn't put a name to this closeness, but I didn't care. I just liked it and I was content.

"I'm sorry," Rhein finally said, "I shouldn't have reacted like this. I've ruined your day."

"No, you haven't. You're just tired. I, as well, am tired. If you hadn't come to offer me a tour, I would've thrown all those new vials of steam out the window. You actually saved my day."

Rhein coughed a laugh, which meant I had managed to calm him.

"We have been working really hard," Rhein agreed.

Bubbles, how true that was. We had been very busy, working for months, securing every important location in the city, from the steam factory to the market and the farm. One would think after winning a big battle, things would ease up and we'd have a bit of peace, but nope, the amount of work doubled. Soldiers were tasked with weeding out spies, inventors had to come up with new ideas and Burk and I were doing our best to enhance Paiza's magic in order to figure out the old ancient spell to create the one-of-a-kind steam. This was all because other cities and kingdoms were capable of attacking Paiza, including the Court of Wizards.

It was a lot to deal with.

"Still, I'm happy," I admitted. "I liked being busy, especially on those days when all I could think about was the Court of Wizards." I liked the distraction and the satisfaction of helping.

"I am too," he smiled and held my hand up to his lips.

Suddenly, the door behind us crashed opened, causing us both to jump to our feet.

Hexing bubbles! Couldn't people leave us alone?

Standing at the door was the young inventor I'd saved. He didn't meet my eyes and his face was as red as his hair.

"Here," he almost whispered, offering me a small metal rock that glimmered under the sun. "It's cobalt. For saving me."

"Oh, thank you," I said, taking it and smiling wide at the inventor. He nodded sheepishly, ruffled his hair and left in a hurry.

"That is one rare metal. Your admirers are growing in numbers," Rhein remarked.

"The perks of being Paiza's protector," I replied with a giggle.

With a swift assertive move, Rhein turned me to face him. His hands firm on my waist, holding me close. My breath shallowed and my head felt light.

"But who does the protector admire?" he whispered. His warm breath tickling my nose, sending shivers down my spine. Life around us was muffled by the sound of my thunderous heartbeat.

"Oh, is the King of Paiza jealous?" I said, humming, teasing him and enjoying how his fingers dug into my waist as he got impatient waiting for me to say his name.

"Who?" he urged me as a chilly breeze danced around us.

"There is one. His name is ..." I paused for only a second, only to say the name he longed to hear, "Rhein."

CHAPTER 2

Bubbles, how exhausted I felt.

I sighed and sunk deeper in my warm copper tub. The water soothed my aching muscles. After my whining in the factory, Burk thought I needed a day without work. A day where I could finally rest. I welcomed it. I felt like we had been running from one place to the next for months. I didn't mind it though. It was a summer I would never forget.

I stared at the ceiling that was filled with lines of copper pipes, bringing in the hot and cold water and admired the tiny patches of moss hiding in any damp nook and cranny. It was so wonderful how nature and machinery interweaved together creating this beautiful new harmony of life. I breathed in the quietness of the moment and breathed out, releasing my powers.

Purple bubbles formed on the waters and like clouds, they floated around me, shimmering with hidden tiny stars. I hummed a melody Chi taught me during our work on the farm. The bubbles dancing with every tune.

"Tia! Tia!" Anna's voice burst into my room, cutting my calming thoughts. Fear rushed through my heart, making me jump up. Water spilled over the ceramic tub and into the stone floor with a soft splash.

I ran out of the washroom. My robe flew and covered my body. In my room, I found Anna standing by the table. Her face, framed by her golden long curls, was totally stunned.

"Bubbles, Anna. What's wrong?" I said urging her to speak. She was wearing her pink dress with her cloak, so she must have come from outside the castle.

"Is it Rhein? Has something happened?" I said, losing my patience. "For bubble's sake, Anna! Speak!"

"I … I have been promised," she said so softly as if she didn't believe a word she was saying.

I frowned in confusion as she held out a golden coin. I squinted at it, wondering what was so special about it, before noticing that it wasn't like the coins we normally use to buy things. It was still made with gold, but unlike the normal gear symbol embossed on it, this coin had a carving of a flaming sun with a tiny carved heart in its center.

"I have been promised," Anna repeated, waiting for me to react and I was so confused. Was I supposed to be happy, sad, angry or what?

"What does that mean?" I asked, my voice failing to conceal how irritated I was getting. My heart was still recovering from the fright of her shouting calls.

"Dryx and I are getting married!" she exclaimed.

I blinked, not fully comprehending what she was saying, but with another blink, it hit me.

I squealed and Anna squealed as I threw my arms around her.

"Hexing cauldrons, Anna!" I said letting her go. "You scared the bubbles out of me."

"Oh, don't be dramatic. How else could I have reacted? You have no idea how much it took of me to hold my excitement from the market until I saw you."

I rolled my eyes. *I'm the one who's dramatic?*

"So, what's with the coin?"

"Oh, didn't you use them where you used to live?"

I shook my head. People rarely got married there.

"This is a promise coin," she explained, handing the coin to me. "When a man wishes to marry a woman, he offers her a specially designed coin, just for her. If she accepts the coin, it means she will marry him. If she doesn't, well it'll be an awkward day for the guy. The coin can be made with any metal, but what matter is the symbol carved in it."

"Oh, interesting," I said admiring the details.

"Maybe one day, soon, you will get yours," she winked and, again, it took me a moment to understand what she meant.

This time, I was the one who was stunned, as I shoved the coin back at her. How silly of her to even suggest it. Marriage? Me?

"I bet his majesty will make you the most wonderful coin," Anna said with a twinkle in her eyes that made me extremely uncomfortable.

"You know what? I am very hungry. Let's go find something to eat," I said and before Anna could add another preposterous suggestion, I wielded my powers. A gust of sparkling wind twirled around me, replacing the robe with my green cotton dress.

"You are *so* going to make my wedding dress," Anna said as we left my room.

"Oh, bubbles yes!" I exclaimed, excitedly. I would make her the most wonderfully magical wedding dress ever made.

"But don't you think, the three dots will be upset?" I added as we climbed down the tower. "I mean, it is their profession and you are their loyal customer."

"Well, we can figure something out," said Anna, who was pursing her lips in thought. "Perhaps, you can work with them. They can ..." she stopped and wrinkled her nose, "what is that smell?"

I sniffed and gagged. A vile smell burned my nostrils as we entered the workshop.

"By the mountain! Burk!" Anna gasped at the sight of him, standing in the middle of the workshop, drenched in mud. A puddle of more mud, rocks and dried leaves drowned his feet and the carpet.

"Ah, do not worry, my dear. Just another day in the life of the court's magician," he said in his theatrical tone while spreading his arms wide, splashing the place with mud.

"Be careful, Burk," I said as I was hit by the splatter.

"Ah, sorry child. May I ask for your quick assistance?" he said, apologetically.

"Of course," I raised both my hands, my palms directed at Burk and released my powers. The light from my hand latched onto the mud, taking it all from his body and the floor and creating a ball of brownish goo that floated above us. When the last dot of mud was removed and squished into the ball, I beckoned it to move.

Anna, understanding what I was doing, ran and opened the door just before the ball of goo shot out of it, heading to the courtyard where I allowed it to flop.

Burk would still need a bath, but when I dropped my hands, he was back to normal. Well, as normal as Burk could be.

"What happened?" I asked. I knew he was working on the farm that day, but from what I understood from him, it was just a normal spell checkup. He assured me that it would not require my help. Clearly, he was wrong.

"An unexpected surge in the mountain's magic led to a small mud slide. I managed to stop it, but somehow I was transferred here." Burk blinked and looked around us as if he wanted to make sure that he was truly with us at the workshop.

"Is something wrong with the magic? Is it the farm?" I asked, frowning.

"Is it an attack?" Anna said, which was her new response whenever something went wrong in the city during the summer. Even if it was just a small accident, she would jump to the conclusion that it was an attack. No matter how much I assured her that Thaiba, the neighboring city that literally tried to kill the King and invade the city last spring, were not capable of doing anything to hurt us anymore.

"It is just an anomaly. Nothing to worry about. It has happened before," Burk said waving his hand, dismissing our concerns. Yet, living with this eccentric wizard for the past few months had taught me the signs of his true reactions, no matter how subtle. From what I could tell from the soft crease in his eyes, this specific anomaly did not happen very often.

"So, what were you two ladies talking about?" he said with his widest smile.

"How Tia is going to make my wedding dress," Anna said, taking the opportunity to show her coin again. Her fear of an attack replaced with the delight of seeing Burk's joyful surprised face.

"A wedding! Oh, how wonderful!" Burk said, taking Anna's arm in his, "You must tell me all about it."

He led her to the dining table, as Anna described how Dryx took her to a beautifully secluded garden and presented her with the coin.

I stared at them as Anna continued discussing the poem Dryx wrote her. I began to feel a whisper of dread rising in the back of my mind.

Something was wrong, I could feel it, but I didn't know what. I shrugged. Until I figured it out, we had a wedding to plan.

CHAPTER 3

"Hex!" I jolted up. Every limb in me shaking. My right hand clutched my left arm. Something stung me. The pain, which was too real to be a dream, was so sharp it woke me up.

It was a dark moonless night. I knew I was in my room, but what had happened? *Why am I in pain?*

Panting, I wielded three balls of purple flame and lit the room around me. There was no-one there that could have attacked me. I could sense no magic. There was nothing that could've caused the pain. I looked down at my left arm and my hand. *Bubbles!* My fingers were covered in electric sparks.

Did I hurt myself? My mind immediately recalled the day at the factory and how a sharp pain also hit the same arm. I thought it happened because I had spent all day casting that steam spell.

I stretched my left arm and massaged it. Was this a reaction to the spell? Burk did just guess how it was supposed to be casted. Or perhaps I was exhausting my powers?

I had never used this much power in such a short period of time before. Even back at that wretched court, the high members would ask me - actually, more like command me - to help with a spell or potion that required a large portion of my powers.

But that was like once every fortnight or every month, and with spells far less powerful. Yes, my body was probably overwhelmed by all the magic I had used these past few months. I should ask for more resting days from Burk in the morning.

I hugged my pillow and took a few deep breaths to calm my nerves.

"I need tea," I whispered and slid off the bed, throwing the pillow back to its place. I grabbed my purple cloak as I headed downstairs.

I rarely ever went down to the workshop this late but as I walked into the circular hall, I felt the warmth of the fire and saw its faint glow dancing around the walls; it mesmerized me. A hum came from a big cauldron hovering above the fire; a potion was left to brew overnight.

I walked to the wall of materials and stared at the shelf-covered wall that housed all the jars. My eyes trailed the line of herbs and magical items, before reaching for the lavender jar.

Bubbles! The jar was empty. Burk must've used the whole patch for one of his potions. I looked around helplessly. I really needed something to help me sleep and there was only one thing to be done now. *Go to the kitchen.*

There was probably no-one there at this hour and that would be the only reason that helped me muster enough courage to go there. Since I arrived in Paiza, I always had the sense that the Head Cook Gib hated me. A fact that his narrowed angry eyes told me, every time I met him, but it was past midnight and Gib was probably fast asleep.

I clutched the empty jar to my chest, nodded and walked out of the workshop, through the dark corridor and down the stairway that led to the kitchen. I took one soft barefooted step at a time, as stealthily as a cat. I could hear tinkering noises trickling up the stairs from the kitchen.

The oven? Or a machine left working overnight to prepare something for tomorrow, like our cauldron? I hoped it was the potato slicer. Midnight fried potatoes sounded so delicious.

I peeked my head through the entrance. The cave of culinary wonder was empty, no soul in sight. I walked in and passed the spotless wooden tables and rows of iron stoves, pouting as I couldn't locate potato slices anywhere. The soft buzz of the big iron cubes, called fridges and the softness of the ceiling lamps made me sleepy. Oh well, I would just get the lavender and head back to bed. I moved toward the storage room at the end of the kitchen cave, where the ingredients were kept, when -

"Ah!" I yelled as my whole body slammed against the cold stone ground.

A bang sounded behind me, followed by a muffled groan as I turned, wincing at a pain in my elbow.

"What in the bubbles?!" I cursed at the sight of a man who had half of his body stuck inside an oven and half laid on the floor; the half I had tripped over.

"Why in the hexing cauldrons are you sleeping in an oven, sir?" I snapped at him.

The man slipped out of the oven, rubbing his head. His face was smeared with grease, but I still recognized him. *Rhein.*

"I should've guessed it was you, Purple Hair," he said with a smile. "You made me bang my head."

"Well, you made me hurt my elbow," I said rubbing it.

"I did?" he frowned in genuine concern and reached for my hand. A shiver ran down my spine and my stomach curled as he pushed my cloak away and examined my arm. He leaned closer. Our bodies were close, so close, I couldn't take it.

"There's no mark thankfully," he said, his hand still on my arm.

"Well, I heal really fast," I said, as I reached for his face. My fingers touched his scar, brushing over the rough skin. It was something I once offended him with, yet, it was the past pain that bonded us. I might not have an obvious scar like his, but I have my own, hiding deep in the darkness. He leaned into my touch, his lips grazing my palm, as he whispered, "I bet you do, Purple Hair."

I felt all my anxiousness and sleep deprivation vanish before a sudden whizzing and clicking noise emerged from the same oven Rhein was tinkering with.

"What is that?" I said pulling my hand away.

"That," Rhein's eyes flashed with excitement as he reached inside the oven and pulled a bronze triangle and an iron box out of the oven, "is my new engine."

"Did you invent it?" I said, grinning at the smile that lit his face as he nodded, "Can I see it?"

He coughed a laugh and leaned forward, "Yes, but you have to promise …"

"Bubbles! Yes, yes, I will not destroy it," I said; my heart could've grown wings at the sound of his laugh.

"It happened once!" I said, referring to the time I had to throw a music box he made for me in a boiling cauldron to find the man who attacked him. "And it was to save your life. So, you have to let it go."

"Alright, here you go," he laughed, handing it to me. It fit in the palms of my hands and upon closer inspection I could see tiny gears moving inside, whilst pipes and metal needles stuck out from the top. I never understood Rhein's gadgets, but I loved the glint in his eyes that shone, whenever he talked about his inventions. That glint told me he was happy.

"It's so tiny," I said, squinting.

"That's the point. If I could reduce the engine's size, we could achieve so much," Rhein said, taking the engine from my hand with such care, which showed how important this project was to him.

"The problem is this," he pointed at two tiny golden valves attached to the engine's side. "See how small those valves are? Iron and copper pipes would not work with these. I need a more flexible material."

"Like fabric? Oh! Animal skin?" I said excitedly as if I'd solved his problem.

"Yes! Something like that," he said, excitedly that I knew what he meant. "But a sturdier material, something that will survive for years. Chi and I have already started experimenting …" he began explaining the process of making this new material. He said a lot of words that I didn't know. He often told me things about his gadgets that I didn't understand, but I didn't mind. I liked just hearing him talk in that happy tone of his.

He blinked in the middle of a sentence, probably realizing he was rambling on.

Rhein cleared his throat, "Anyway," he said, as his face turned to a soft shade of pink whilst he returned the engine to its wooden box and packed up his tools. "Why are you still awake?"

"Nightmares," I lied, as I handed him a hammer, I found next to me. I couldn't tell him I attacked myself. No need to worry him. Not until I figured out what was wrong.

"I have those too," he said with a gentle smile. "What are yours about?"

"Slimy corpses crawling from under my bed or jumping out of my wardrobe," I added to the lie. Though, it was only half a lie, I did have those dreams more than once. They were the same stinky corpses I had to fight at the battle of the wall, "You?"

"Broken gadgets, ruining things," he smiled but the glint in his eyes disappeared.

"They are just dreams. Our minds trying to trick us," I said, reaching for his hand. He nodded, his thumb brushing my wrist.

"I thought lavender tea would help me sleep," I added cheerily.

"Then allow me to assist you with that," he said, rising to his feet.

"Wait, you, the King of Paiza will *me* make tea?!" I chuckled in surprise as I watched him walk to the storage room.

"Yes, and it will be the best tea you've ever had."

I giggled, wrapping my cloak tighter around me, as he disappeared into the room. The way he said 'broken gadgets and ruining things' stirred a new doubt inside me. What if my magic *was* broken? Was that even possible? I groaned and felt the sickness of anxiety take hold of me, but *hexing bubbles*, this was a rare moment I could spend alone with Rhein. I would not ruin it with dark thoughts. I would deal with it in the morning. *Keep it together, Tia!*

Other than the morning of the battle, we spent one day together without guards or servants hovering around us. I was resting in my room when he brought me the sugar covered dough from the market and we just sat, ate and talked about so many random things. It was a beautiful day until he was called away for his royal duties. He was always being called away, which saddened more often than I would like to admit.

Rhein came back carrying a couple of jars, half a loaf of bread and an iron kettle. He placed the jars on a wooden table and took the kettle to a basin to wash it. I sat on a wooden stool as I watched him clean the kettle, fill it with clean water from a faucet and put it on a stove.

He then picked a glass off the shelf and opened a jar of honey. As he poured the golden liquid into the glass, he looked up and winked at me and I failed to hold back a giggle. Something about us being together felt right. I felt as if I had found the place I'd been looking for my whole life; a place where I was safe to be myself.

"You know your way around the kitchen," I said as Rhein sliced two pieces of bread and spread a layer of honey on them before handing me one.

"I used to come here all the time when I couldn't sleep. I would diassemble a machine, then try to reassemble it," he said, biting his slice, "I was the cause of changing that line of fridges at one point."

"All of them? One wasn't enough?"

"Well, I needed to understand how the mechanics worked. I had to make sure I wasn't missing any details."

"Oh, I bet Gib is still holding a grudge."

"No, no. He was actually happy. He was hoping for replacements, and I made it happen," he smirked at me, and I wanted to melt.

The kettle whistled and with one swift move, he picked it up and poured the hot water into two cups holding a strainer filled with lavender buds. I admired his grace and how meticulous he was, like this cup of tea was an important invention.

It amazed me how different he was now to the days we first met. How cold and intimidating he was. Even to me. But not anymore. Not since he started inventing again. He was still cautious and scheduled everything to the minute, but there was a warmth and an underlying joy that shined from his eyes. How life changed us; or perhaps life just lead us back to who we truly are?

"Your tea, my lady," Rhein said in a jokingly formal tone as he handed me the glass and the blended smell of honey and lavender revived my soul.

"Oh, thank you, your Majesty," I echoed his tone with a giggle.

"Wait, there is one more thing," he pulled something from his pocket. It was two springs of lavender.

"May I?" he said, and I nodded.

He leaned closer and his hands reached for my hair. Bubbles, that tickled. I failed again to hold back a giggle. Oh, I could get used to him pampering me.

"Now you may drink your tea," he said leaning back, smiling wide, happy with how the lavender looked in my hair. I felt heat rise within my cheeks.

"I miss you," he said in the softest of whispers.

Oh, to hear those words from him. *Bubbles,* I felt as if my heart would halt... *Say you miss him too!* But I just smiled, awkwardly and took a sip of the tea. *Bubbles!*

"Oh, this is the best tea," I said, closing my eyes. I breathed in the calming scent of the lavender and it brought warmth to my heart. Opening my eyes, I let myself be taken by Rhein, by his energy, the tilt of his smile, the sharpness of his scar, the darkness of his hair and by my favorite, the endless fog of those gray eyes. I was falling for the King of Paiza and I did not know how to handle it. I used to deny it at first, scared of wishing for more, for wanting more than just hiding in this city. But after the battle my feelings for him intensified and I didn't know how to deal with it. All I knew was, I wanted more.

"I missed you too, like a lot," I blurted in the silence.

"You missed me a lot?" Rhein said, leaning closer. Butterflies fluttered inside of me at the feeling of his warm lips on my cheek. He moved to my other cheek when-

"Bubbles!" I cursed.

Rhein alertly turned to see what startled me, only to sigh and relax at the sight of four guards eyeing him as if he was caught stealing something.

"Ah, we have been caught," Rhein said, smiling. The kind of smile that reached his eyes, not the shadow of a smile he normally showed. I so wanted to hug him. *Hexing guards.*

"When did you start having guards follow you around?" I whispered to him, trying not to look any of them in the eyes.

"My uncle insisted on bringing back the king's guards. I don't have much protection after the ring broke." My hand reached for the pale band of skin on one of his fingers where the ring used to be.

Before the battle of the wall, Rhein possessed a magical ring that protected him by projecting a strong magical shield around him whenever it sensed danger. The ring was destroyed a couple of days before the battle.

"I prefer the guards over the ring," I said frowning at his hand.

"Though it was nice having a piece of you with me," he replied.

I frowned deeper and this time he realized he said the wrong thing as he cleared his throat and nodded at the guards.

"We should rest," he said, picking up his bag of tools.

I sighed and nodded, hating this awkward moment as he reached for my hand. I took it and leaned on him, as he led me back to my tower.

Climbing the stairs up to my tower with Rhein by my side, I was packed with joy and fuzziness, hugging my warm cup, hopeful.

"Good night, Purple Hair," he leaned to kiss my star tattoo, ignoring the group of guards still tailing us and filling me with joy. Watching him go, I decided that I would allow myself to be with Rhein and accept my happiness in Paiza.

Little did I know, darkness was closer than I thought.

CHAPTER 4

"You will be joining me today at the court's gathering this afternoon," Burk suddenly announced in the middle of what was a very quiet breakfast.

"Why?" I asked with a yawn. Even after revealing my true powers during the battle of the wall and becoming *the* protector, I still spent most of my days at the workshop or at the farm helping Chi. I rarely ever attended court gatherings. I never enjoyed it. It was basically people drinking sparkly drinks and talking about the same things. They talked about the battle of the wall and doted on me as the protector, before returning to their favorite subject, steam fashion.

"For court magician business," Burk said, averting his eyes.

"But why do *I* need to be there? You always go by yourself and told me what I needed to do."

"This time, you must," he said, clearing his throat as he tapped his fingers lightly on the table.

He is hiding something.

"Now," Burk stood up, all flustered, "I have to attend to an important matter in the *err* kitchen."

He sprinted to the door, yelling, "I expect you to be at the court hall at four, sharp!" and disappeared down the corridor before I could say anything.

Bubbles. I breathed out and took a bite out my toast.

***

I rested my palm on one of the empty spaces in our workshop's walls. The surface was smooth, cool and I sent my magic through it, calling for a door. Yes, I had finally managed to crack the secret of the vanishing doors. The doors that could take me from the workshop to any part of the castle in one step.

It turned out that the castle was basically alive with magic, just like the mountain. But unlike the mountain, which was solely linked to the shimmering steam, the castle's magic was pure, ancient and had a will of its own. It was as if it was a real person with a soul. A soul that hid itself from me.

"The castle is very wary of strangers," Burk told me once, "but now, you're a Paizan. You are one of us."

Nothing in my life had anchored my soul like those words did. I had finally found a place where I belonged and thus the castle revealed its magic and allowed me to call upon those doors.

"The court hall," I whispered and like a rippling mirage, the door manifested before me.

I held the knob and was about to turn it, before hearing a familiar voice with a disgusted tone.

"Oh, you are so not going to the gathering wearing that!" Anna said with a very judgmental glare, walking into the workshop.

"What do you mean, 'wearing that?' This is a new working dress," I said, my hand unconsciously brushing the soft peach cotton fabric.

"Exactly. You look like you were going to pick herbs from the gardens," she said, hands on hips.

"Burk told me we were going on magician business."

"Oh, that man is hopeless. This dress is too simple. Not for the court and not for today."

I grabbed her hand, "You know something! Tell me!"

"I will not tell you. All I shall say is that this dress is too simple."

"Bubbles, I hate surprises." I huffed in frustration and flicked my wrist. The fabric transfigured from cotton to silk that rippled around my body like waves.

"Still too simple" Anna said, folding her arms in discontent.

Bubbles, how the Paizans loved their fashion.

I grumbled and tightened my fists. When I opened them, a pile of tiny crystals appeared, floated off my hand and landed across the dress. I closed my hand again, as the new pile of crystals flew to my head, with each finding a curl to rest on.

"Ah, that's better," Anna chirped, as she smiled widely at my transformation into a walking chandelier.

"May I go now?" I said shaking my head in defeat.

"Yes, you shouldn't be late, and you better tell me everything later!"

"I will," I rolled my eyes, knowing she would sneak into the hall as usual and learn everything herself, and turned the knob.

Within a blink, I stepped into the lavish marble corridor. The door vanished behind me as I walked into the hall. I kept my head high trying to breathe. I knew that nothing evil or menacing was waiting for me there, but I hated not knowing what this whole thing was all about. If it was about me, which I guessed it was from Burk and Anna's behavior, I didn't want to go. I hated being the center of everyone's attention. It terrified me.

Getting closer to the door and hearing the chatter of the courtiers inside, my stomach felt as heavy as iron. I wanted to run and hide in the comfort of our workshop, but I tried to ease my anxiousness and reminded myself, that Burk was there and Rhein would probably be there soon.

I took a deep breath and stepped into the hall.

"Lady Datia, Wielder of Stars and Protector of Paiza," I flinched as a page announced my entrance. Everyone's eyes turned toward me. Oh, this gathering was *definitely* about me.

I took a step back, ready to retreat when Lord Byron appeared before me, standing in all his fashionable glory. He wore a dark brown fitted suit that had a shimmer of green dancing across it, visible to those who squinted hard enough. Copper pins in the shape of leaves adorned his chest and arms, yet his fair hair was a bit darker, like the color of burned gold. He was autumn incarnate.

"Tia, darling," he said with his dashing smile and sparkling blue eyes. Before I could greet him, he took my arm in his and led me to the middle of the hall. His presence somehow grounded me.

"Please tell me you know what is going on," I whispered to him, tugging his arm as we walked between more staring eyes.

"Oh, of course I know."

"Well, what is it?" I urged him.

"And spoil the surprise? My cousin would have me hanged."

"Ah, you're all so stubborn," I said which made Byron laugh.

"Have some patience, Tia, darling and allow my cousin this joy."

You'll have your coin soon. Anna's voice whispered in my mind and panic wrapped its rope around my lungs. This couldn't be. This was happening too soon. We still hadn't had much time alone together. Shouldn't we know each other more or was this normal here in Paiza with marriage promises? Anna knew Dryx for as long as I knew Rhein, but they spent every free moment together.

Bubbles! What did I even know about marriage anyway? My parents gave me away to the court when I was just a tiny baby. I don't even remember them and growing up at the court didn't give me any sense of what marriage could be like. No-one cared about this type of marital bond. There was no concept of family there. There was no need. We were never short of children, because so many people had sent their kids to the court hoping for better lives as callers or from the fear of their wielding magic. We were raised together as children until we reached a certain age then were all sent off to work for the court.

Which type were my parents? The hopeful or the afraid? I never knew and never asked.

All I wanted was to break free from the high members. I had never considered the possibility of having my own family! But now, not only was there a possibility of me having that family but there was also the possibility of becoming a queen. *A queen!* Hexing bubbles! As if I needed a new title added to my name!

"Tia, darling, are you alright?" Byron's hand touched mine and I blinked at him, noticing that he was frowning, "You look like you've inhaled a tube of steam. Between us, I did inhale it once," the frown turned to a cheeky smirk as he told me all about that day. I couldn't focus on anything he was saying as I noticed the court page had walked toward us and boomed,

"His Royal Majesty, King Rhein. His Royal Highness, Lord Rowen and His Grace, the Court Magician, Burk."

Everyone fell silent as Rhein walked in and my heart fell to my knees as every nerve in me shook at the sight of his gold and emerald crown resting on his dark hair. He never wore the crown, unless ... *Oh, cursed pixies!* Burk followed him wearing his lavish green suit with the green hat. The one with the feather.

Bubbles and hexes. This was too formal. This was too important.

Could it be? My throat closed in onto itself. *No, no it couldn't.*

Rhein winked at me as he passed us on his way to his chair. Byron winced beside me as my finger dug deep into his arm.

"As you all know, Summer is at its end and our tradition dictates that we welcome autumn with our annual Falling Leaves Festival," Rhein started his speech, standing with the throne behind him.

People clapped and Byron whooped which put a wide smile on Rhein's normally very serious face. My heart melted and the tension in my limbs eased a bit. Maybe it wasn't so bad to be his queen. To live here among friends and finally have a family.

"And with that, I have an announcement. Our theme for this festival is … Burk if I may," Rhein waved at him.

Theme?

Burk in his normal waltzing grace floating toward the King, holding the box high for people to see. Made with redwood, the box was carved with tens of tiny leaves and had silver latches on its corners. Rhein took the box from him and placed it on a table that one of the servants brought without us noticing.

The King pressed a button on this mystery object and with a click, the lid popped open. Purple light shot out of it like fireworks and created five glittering stars that flew above us, casting a purple hue across the hall. People gasped in awe as a new ripple of applause erupted.

"Purple stars, to honor our protector," Rhein said, looking directly at me. *What in the bubbles?* My cheeks felt flushed as the way he gazed at me made everyone around us vanish. It was as if it was only him and I in that hall.

Someone nudged me, probably Byron and I step forward toward Rhein. With everyone's eyes on me again, I could feel how they approved this choice. Well, of course, there was the jab of jealousy from one or two people, but the majority were happy, and their kindness eased all the anxiety in me. I was among my people, and I shouldn't be afraid of their attention.

Rhein took my hand, and his lips grazed my knuckles in a gentle kiss. My skin burned with the touch.

A servant appeared holding two glasses of sparkling cider. Rhein took the glasses and handed me one.

"To our Purple Star. May she lead us into a path full of light," Rhein said loud enough for the whole hall to hear. His eyes glimmered with joy as he sipped his drink. People cheered and drank.

I held my glass up to my lips and let the drink cool me down, relieved that the news about me was just that. There was no promise and no coin. It was only me taking Anna's words too seriously and and letting it mess with my mind. It was only a fun celebration.

Rhein had his hand on my waist and through all the relief and joy of knowing the surprise, I couldn't help but feel a tiny, very tiny, bit disappointed.

CHAPTER 5

"Please allow me to help," I said with a bit of a whine to Burk who was standing in front of one of our largest cauldrons. He mumbled an incantation as he stirred whatever potion he was making with a wooden spoon made for giants.

"No, no. This year's festival will celebrate you and all that you have done for us," he said, waving one hand to dismiss me, while the other kept stirring. "Letting you help will ruin the many surprises I have planned for you."

From the objects scattered around the workshop, I could guess a few surprises already, but Burk was so jolly and thrilled with all the Falling Leaves Festival preparations, I played along making him think I was clueless.

"Alright, fine, but don't you have any other tasks you can give me? Anything random. I could make a new headache begone patch?" I said clasping my hands together, literally begging. I was fine with resting for a couple of days, but to have a full week of doing nothing was taking me to dark thoughts. Yes, Paiza was super secure with everything we did during the summer, but I still needed to work. I used to be a high member of the Court of Wizards, for bubbling cauldron's sake! Being the *theme* of a festival didn't make me a fragile crystal.

Burk sighed, let go of the spoon and turned toward me. He took my clasped fist in his hands and looked at me with his kind nurse frown.

"Child," he said, "you have faced so much hardship, for many years." His words stirred something in my heart that clawed at old wounds. "Allow us to be kind to you. Just this once. Can you promise me that?" His eyes filled with sympathy. It was as if he wanted to say, let's have fun now, because new hardship could knock on our doors any moment. The image of Burk covered in mud passed before me. Shadows crept in the back of my mind, but I pushed them away.

Burk was right. There was no harm in enjoying this festive season. I nodded and pulled my hand away from him. He gave me one more frown of sympathy and turned to his cauldron. A wide smile replacing all the concern on his face.

I smiled and sat at the table. Burk would always be Burk and that was comforting.

I tried to read a book but managed only to pile a collection of unread books on the table. My fingers played with my curls, twisting and untwisting them as I watched Burk move from one spell to the next.

"Burk, what does the Falling Leaves Festival normally celebrate?" I said, loudly to get his attention.

"Ah, it celebrates the changing of seasons and pays tribute to the mountain for all the blessings it provides us. It represents our wish for a safe and peaceful winter. Hence why you are one of those blessings."

"That is beautiful."

Burk hummed a cheerful tone and a word or two escaped him now and then. Words about autumn and the mountain.

I thought of the festival and how fun it would be. I thought of autumn in Paiza. I bet this city would be even more beautiful with the trees changing color to gold, brown and even shades of purple. The city was glowing already with its copper braces and mechanical pipes, but the changing of leaves would add another layer to its charm.

"I don't pay you to nap all day, Purple Hair."

I lifted my head, smiling. *Rhein.*

"Tell that to Burk," I said, pointing at the humming magician with his cauldron behind me.

"Hey," Rhein said with his crooked smile. Ah, how casual yet very charming, he was standing by the table, in his black outfit. His watch hidden as usual in his pocket and his black sleeves rolled up; a sign he'd had a busy day. The King of Paiza, with his mesmerizing gray eyes and smile, was exactly what I needed to cheer me up.

"Hi," I said, trying to calm the flutters in my stomach, "I didn't expect a visit today."

"Well, I am allowed to break my schedule once in a while," he said with a wink before summoning Burk.

Oh, so he wasn't here for me.

"Your Majesty!" Burk beamed, stopping his humming and potion stirring.

Rhein walked to him and handed him a piece of paper. Burk bowed slightly and his cheerfulness faded as he took it.

Burk nodded and left the boiling potion with its giant spoon stirring on its own to create something new. Rhein returned to sit by my side as Burk fumbled around the workshop, picking up jars and settling down a smaller cauldron on the fire, preparing whatever potion the King needed.

"Will you have lunch with me?" I said trying to squeeze myself into his plans.

"Sadly, I can't. I have a meeting with the emissary of Kab in a few minutes," he said, as his cold gaze sliced my heart in half.

"Emissaries and ambassadors keep visiting you. Is everything alright?"

"Yes, it's all good," he said, softening his features, "everyone just needs reassurance that our production of steam had not been compromised by the attack and that we are not suspecting them to be cooperating with Thaiba."

"It's ready!" Burk boomed, holding up a vile of something green. From the smell that now filled the workshop I recognized that potion. It was a sleeping draught. A very heavy one. *Was it for him?*

"Tia," Rhein said, cutting my train of thought. I reached for his chest, my fingers holding the silver thread that held his pocket watch. I was worried.

"At the end of the Falling Leaves Festival, would you meet me at the clock tower?" his fingers brushed the star under my eyes. "We can watch the fireworks and …" I looked up at him, his eyes were intense. Tiny wrinkles formed between his eyebrows. "I want to tell you something."

"Another announcement?"

"Something like that."

"You know you can tell me now," I said, my fingers brushing his arm.

Rhein brushed his hair back and leered at me sarcastically. "You shall not trick me, sorceress."

"Alright, I'll wait," I said with an eye roll to match his sarcasm. "Sadly, I have nothing else to do."

"Sadly?" he coughed a laugh. "Is it such a boring affair to wait for a special evening with the King?"

"Oh, bubbles, no. I didn't mean it that way," *rusty cauldron, get it together*, "it's just Burk keeps refusing my help. I have nothing to do all day. I didn't mean spending time with you wasn't good enough. It's the best actually."

"Really? The best?" He gave my hand a squeeze and his lips brushed my cheeks in a quick kiss.

"Ahem, your Majesty? What about your meeting?" Burk said, making Rhein lean back and ending our moment. I swore I was going to throttle Burk one day.

"I'll see you later, Purple Hair," he gave my hand one final squeeze and left the workshop.

Burk returned to the potion in the huge cauldron, and I stood there staring at the door which had Rhein just passed through, with the idea of our alone time during the festival simultaneously thrilling and frightening.

***

"The King is going to promise you!" Anna said in the highest of pitches in the middle of a jewelry shop.

"Bubbles Anna! Keep it down," I hissed, pulling her behind the columns of earrings. They were tall and rotated slowly, enough to reflect the sun rays from the wide window and distract the buyers from seeing us.

The shop, which was located in the middle of the market, was busy with buyers who were looking for the best piece to make them stand out during the festival. The place was smaller than the three dots building, but it had enough space to hold a few nosey buyers who could hear what Anna just blurted.

"I'm sorry, but I can't help being excited," Anna said in a hushed tone. "You should've known better than to tell me this in public!"

"Well, you didn't give me a chance to tell you when I saw you this morning. You just listed all the things we had to buy today which literally took the entire walk from the castle to here," I said as I untangled my bag of sweets from the rotating wheel of necklaces on my left. *Why does everything move in this city?*

"I am very excited. It's long overdue too. I really thought he was going to present you the coin at court the other day. Damn Burk was super vague," she said giddily; her eyes shone with so much possibility.

"Perhaps you are wrong again," I argued.

"I am never wrong," she huffed at me, "I may have gotten the day wrong. But I am not wrong about a coin coming your way. I should've also thought about the fact that it would be very boring to promise you in the castle. I mean that's like your house. So lazy. No. The festival with everyone all dressed up and the glimmering magic of the fireworks, now that's a promise fit for a king."

"What? No, he … well …" I trailed off not knowing what to say.

"Think about it, Tia, why else would he ask you to meet him during the most romantic time of the festival??"

"I don't know. There are a million other reasons. I actually think he wants my help with a project he is working on with Chi," I said. Rhein seemed nervous, not happy and in love. He wanted to talk to me about a problem he needed my help with. I was sure of that.

"Oh, please," she scoffed, "if it was about strategy or a project, why couldn't he tell you at the castle or ask you to meet him in Chi's workshop?"

Hexing Pixies. What if he *was* planning something romantic? I knew I wanted something more than those fleeting moments together. And yes, I was disappointed during the theme announcement that day at the court gathering. But could I go through with this, for real? This was too quick.

I opened my mouth, then closed it. Frowning. Anna smiled in an 'I won this argument' kind of way.

A woman, who was fiddling with some copper gloves and was too close to us, leaned nearer toward us.

"Can we help you, miss?" Anna said in the most unpolite tone ever.

"I'm sorry, but you're the protector, aren't you? The witch," she whispered, pointing at me. She was an older type of woman, who wore a floral fabric hat that had so many gears stitched on it, it was weighted down enough to almost cover her eyes. She held a basket filled with every type of jewelry in the shape of a leaf. *Making a new hat, I bet.*

"I'm sorry, you've confused her with someone else," Anna said leading me to the door. If people knew I was out and about in the market, a crowd would form. Something Anna and I learned the hard way a month ago.

The woman blocked our path. She curled her very bright red lips, "You have the same star tattoo."

Bubbles! I forgot to change their colors to match my skin tone. The hair I already hid under my scarf.

"A fake," Anna snapped, "we're fans," she then shoved the woman aside and we dashed out of the shop before she said anything else. We didn't stop until we reached the steam shop at the end of the market.

"That was close," I said, tapping my fingers on all my star tattoos, hiding them from view. "Maybe we should go back. She might tell people."

"Tell who? She looked crazy. No one will listen to her," Anna said, facing the reflecting window of the shop and fixing her hair.

"Now," she said returning her focus on me, "we have to prepare for your promise."

"He's *the King*, Anna. A person you told me to be careful of, remember?"

"I know," she said slowly, "but that was before the battle and before I saw how worried he was when you didn't wake up and let's not forget the way you almost fell apart when he was cursed."

"I did *not* almost fall apart," I said, playing with my scarf.

Anna rested her hands on her waist and looked at me. Her knowing eyes burned my soul, pushing me to admit my feelings toward Rhein. I turned my head, avoiding her gaze.

"What I mean is," I said to change the subject, "he is the King and I'm a magician in his court. He is only interested in my powers." *And maybe something a bit more, but was that love?*

"You are more than your powers, Tia. Yes, he is probably interested in your power, but also in the way you make him happy. He is interested in all of you."

"You think I make him happy?" I said, biting my lips. The inventions were what made him happy again. Perhaps, there was a tiny possibility that I shared that responsibility too. Bubbles! Why did I get even more nervous?

"He is a very kind man and a great king, but ever since that accident at the cave, he hadn't smiled, until you came," Anna said squeezing my shoulders, then tapped them. "Now! Let's go to the three dots; they need to take your measurements for the dress."

"What? I'm doing my own dress."

"No, no. You are the guest of honor, you are doing nothing. The dots are all prepared with the designs and fabric. All they need is you."

"That is disappointing."

"Oh, just think about your special meet up with the King," she said with a wink.

I huffed a couple of sarcastic laughs as I followed her around the market. The truth of what she said was daunting on me.

Oh, hexing bubbles. *What if I was really going to be promised?*

CHAPTER 6

The day of the Falling Leaves Festival finally arrived.

I didn't know what was happening, only that it was a whole day event and that it started with a parade. I was very excited.

Anna swarmed my chamber way too early in the morning with two young maids. They woke me up, hurried me into the bath and allowed me a few minutes to have breakfast before propping me before the mirror to get ready. Their excitement was infectious.

And so, there we were standing in the middle of my room; I had my back toward the mirror. I was not allowed to see anything until I was totally ready. One girl helped me with the dress, while the other worked on my curls as Anna perused a collection of jewelry she had laid out on my table.

She was already ready, with her hair pulled up in coils of braids, like a golden crown. A copper pin rested between the layers. A pin of stars and gears intertwined into a crescent. When she moved, her dress, a modest pink silk, flowed around her with such grace, it was like a magical ancient spirit.

"Ah, for the hate of pixies," I waved away one of the papers Burk enchanted to fly around in the festival had somehow flown into my room. I saw Burk making them throughout the week. He couldn't hide them anywhere, bar the workshop, so this was one surprise that he had to spoil, to his dismay. They were in different sizes and colors and there were so many of them. The one that was hovering around me had tiny dots of purple stars and black cauldrons drawn on it. I kept wincing at the sight of the written line on it: "The Magnificent Datia."

"Alright, enough," Anna said, happy with whatever state I was in. "Thank you, girls. You may go and ready yourselves."

The girls beamed and left us with a curtsy. Curtsying to me was something new that everyone was doing after the battle. I was not used to that.

"Here," Anna said handing me a pair of earrings, "I was allowed to borrow a few pieces from the gold shop. I think these suits you best."

They were two simple strings, one with a golden star and the other a golden crescent.

"They're beautiful!"

"And expensive, so remember to give them back after," Anna said as I wore them, "although if I was right about tonight and I'm sure I am, you won't have to give them back."

"Yeah, yeah," I stammered, feeling the heat rise again in my cheeks. I didn't want to think of my meet up with Rhein later. I wanted to be more excited and less nervous.

A knock on the door saved me from Anna adding to that topic.

"Come in," I called at whoever was knocking.

Another maid walked in, curtsied and said, "The court magician says it is time for you to join him."

"Did Burk just send someone to summon you?" Anna questioned, with her hands on her hips, as the maid left.

"Apparently so. We should go," I said slipping into my shoes.

"No, wait. There is one last thing," Anna said, pursing her lips.

"What now?" I couldn't handle any more thoughts about my future or my current state of magical being. I just wanted to eat pastries and dance.

Anna pulled something from her pocket. It was a small bag.

"From me and Dryx," she said handing it to me.

I was confused, but I opened it. Inside the bag, was the most beautiful hair pin. A bronze crescent of gears and stars intertwined in a beautiful blend. It perfectly matched hers.

"Bubbles, Anna. You shouldn't have." Gratitude overwhelmed me. I didn't know what to say or do.

"Ah, please. How else would everyone know that this amazing lady is my friend," Anna said taking it from my hand and finally turning me to face the mirror. She moved my purple curls to the right and pinned it up.

And right there, I saw myself for the first time and *wow* the three dots had outdone themselves. The sleeveless dress was the color of freshly cooked cherry jam. It had a golden crown of threaded stars and leaves that laid across my arms and chest and with it a cape of matching red, draped my back.

"You look absolutely stunning," Anna said, hugging me from behind.

"Don't say that or I will cry." The tears were very close.

"No, no. No crying today." She shook her head stepping away from me. "Today we celebrate."

"Yes, yes," I said taking a deep breath. No time for tears. "Let's go."

We climbed down the stairs together only to find two men in the official Paizian guard's uniform; all earthly-green with the copper gear pin on their chest, waiting for us instead of Burk.

"Is something the matter?" Anna asked, equally confused.

"We have been instructed by His Majesty and the court's magician to escort you to the celebrations," one guard said. His eyes were on the walls behind us. He was way too formal.

"What? Why?" I asked but he didn't reply. I turned to Anna, "Did you know about this?"

"No, Burk wouldn't tell me anything about today. He was afraid I would tell you."

"Yeah, as if you would."

"Alright, go with them. I need to go find Dryx. We will meet in a bit!" Anna said with a final quick hug before leaving me with the two strangers in the workshop.

"Well, then," I said, trying to sound official too, "lead the way, please."

The guards led me down the staircase and out the small gate under our tower. I smiled at the memory of the first day I stepped through these copper bars. I had hidden my curls and wore a simple dress. A metallic bird was on my shoulder. I came to this city wanting a new hideout, something quiet and nice. I smiled at that image. How naïve was I? Expecting that plan to last for more than couple of months. The whole city now knew who I was.

A rain of brown leaves fell around us as we walked across the path.

The guards stopped by the main gates where a mechanical carriage stood. The roofless carriage was decorated with bronze stars and gears that matched my hair pin and had four clear pipes filled with glittering steam on its back, which were attached to a square box, the engine. There were no horses to pull it, but this was Paiza. Obviously, it would work on its own.

The guards stood by the carriage's small door, opened it and offered me their hands to help me get in.

Bubbles. This was actually happening. I was going to a festival that celebrated me. A mix of pride and anxiety twirled in my chest like a whirling tornado. *Rusty cauldron!* What did I get myself into? I was about to hurl with anxiousness when-

"Climb up, Purple Hair. Burk will curse us both if we're late." Rhein said as he climbed into the carriage from the other side.

He sat there with a matching cherry red cape pinned to his shoulder by his three gears pin. His golden and emerald crown rested on his black hair. Finding him sitting there, with a joyful energy pushed away my anxiousness and filled me with such soaring excitement. I was afraid my power would burst out of me in a shower of sparks.

I flinched when the image of that night with the painful sparkles flashed before me. I didn't have any other incident like that after, but I couldn't risk it. I reminded myself to breathe and calm the bubble down.

"What are you doing here?" I asked as I climbed up and sat by his side.

"Did you think I would miss the opportunity of escorting you to the festival?" he said, winking.

I laughed as he started fiddling with the buttons and sticks.

"Alright, hold tight," he said, pushing a stick down. His foot stepping on a pedal.

The carriage moved, clicking and ticking through the streets of Paiza. The beauty of autumn took my breath away as I expected. The moss-covered buildings were adorned by golden leaves and brown branches. The windows decorated with lanterns and pumpkins in different sizes and colors. And of course, Burk's magic was everywhere.

The magic was in the flying flyers, the floating star lanterns and the sparkling flickering butterflies that shone bright even under the sun like a dancing rainbow.

I could hear music and cheering from the market. As we got closer, I noticed other metallic wagons coming from each alley. They were just square boxes on wheels that trotted before us into the center of the celebrations.

Rhein steered the carriage and when we reached the market, the cheers grew louder. Paizans young and old sat around the market and under the clock tower with only enough path for the parade of wagons to pass. Courtiers and high members of society sat on lavished balconies equipped with metallic leaves that acted as fans. Some I saw whispering to each other as we passed. I bet the fact that Rhein was sitting beside me, wearing the same colors would be the gossip of the night.

"Tia!" Someone shouted from above. I looked up and saw a man in a brown suit, an elaborate hat and a line of copper leaves across his chest. *Byron!*

I waved at him. His lady Jane sat next to him. She wore an orange dress and had a crown of leaves on her head. She just nodded at me.

"Would you do the honors?" Rhein said pointing at a button.

"What does it do?" I squinted at it.

"It starts the parade," he said. I could see from the curl of his lips he was trying his best to disguise his excitement.

"Alright, let's start it then," I said, pushing the button.

The wagons all stopped and with a click, the boxes fell apart. The music changed to a more dramatic tone. My heart drummed with excitement as parts of metal expanded from each wagon to form glorious shapes. A big cauldron, a twirling star, a lavish tree and my favorite one, the pumpkin.

Bubbles and magical fairies!

"How?" I breathed.

"I built the mechanics. Burk did the magic," Rhein said, finally letting his excitement show with a very wide smile. I could tell he was so proud of it.

"They're magnificent!" I said, holding his hand.

The wagons kept expanding and more things kept popping in from the sides of each shape. I could feel the magic that moved it. Burk did an amazing job with the spells, and I could tell that the core work was done by the machine itself.

"No wonder Chi was dying to get you back into inventing. You are brilliant," I said to him, in total awe of his talent.

Rhein didn't say anything, but the way he squeezed my hand and didn't let go showed me he appreciated what I said.

The band, who were stationed on a high stage, played upbeat music that rang through the market circle, as people cheered and waved at me and Rhein whilst we passed them. I laughed and waved back. I was blown away by how delighted people were.

Then, something caught my eyes.

"Is their hair purple?" I asked Rhein as we passed two girls sitting on the floor. Both girls and - oh - three boys behind them had also dyed their hair in different shades of purple.

"Yes, and look," he pointed at an old lady with a star tattoo on her neck.

I looked around, this time with more focus and all I could see were the color purple and stars tattoos everywhere. On their faces, their clothes and on whatever they were holding, whether a cup or a flag.

"This is ..." I was speechless.

"You deserve this," Rhein said, leaning closer.

I looked at him and the amount of happiness and delight on his face warmed my heart. Even the harsh line of his scar had somehow softened.

I wrapped my arms in his and let his confidence in me steady my nerves. I was here. This was my home, and I would do whatever was needed to protect it and make it work.

We stopped in the middle of the market and Rhein climbed down before helping me descend. I kept hold of his arm as I didn't know what was expected of me.

People still sat around us. Little girls waved and giggled when I waved back.

Then with a boom, a cloud of golden smoke erupted from the ground to reveal Burk, in all of his glory, covered in gold from head to toe. An outfit that included a golden hat and feather.

"Yes!" I clapped. I loved how the whole of Paiza had been *Burkfied*.

"Ladies and gentlemen," Burk's voice boomed and echoed around, "a round of applause for the Protector of Paiza."

The market erupted and if not for the possibility of Burk killing me for it, I would've disappeared right then and there. This was too much. The attention was too much.

I couldn't breathe. And to make it worse, Rhein let go of my arm and walked away.

No, no. Bubbles! Come back.

I panicked as I watched him walk between the people, but then the panic was replaced with confusion as he jumped on the the band's stage.

"My dear people of Paiza," Rhein said addressing the market. "Yes, today we celebrate our new protector, Datia, Wielder of Stars." *Bubbles*; he pointed at me. "We also celebrate the start of fall and the turning of leaves. We had a hard summer. We were attacked," people booed, "and we have won," cheers erupted again, "and so we celebrate you today, too! Our farmers, soldiers, inventors, bakers, shopkeepers-"

"-Jewelers!" a man shouted.

Rhein laughed, "Yes, all of you, my brothers and sisters. Here's to a new year of fortune and working together to be better and more magical. We are Paiza and nothing defeats us!"

The cheers shook the city and with a wave from Rhein, the band started playing again as, to my relief, people began to move around, to dance, to play and to enjoy the day.

I though, kept my eyes on Rhein and full with gratitude I mouthed, "Thank you."

He didn't leave me alone in the middle of the crowd. No, he left to take the attention away from me and that was the sweetest thing that anyone had ever done for me, and a tingle rushed through my body at the prospect of being alone with him later that evening.

"I didn't finish my speech," Burk said to me flustered.

"You don't have to say anything. Burk, the festival is beautiful!" I said patting his arm. I knew he wanted to have his theater moment. "And look! We match." I pointed at the pin on the chest and my hair pin.

"Yes, Anna gave it to me and told me she will give you something to match it," Burk nodded, still very disappointed that he lost his moment in the sun.

"Show me what other spells you have prepared for me today," I said. I was so happy and relieved to see his eyes sparkle at that request.

"Let's begin the tour!" he clapped and took my hand.

We passed Rhein and I frowned in a *'sorry have to go with him'* way and he nodded at me with his *'I understand'* croaked smile.

And so, the day of the Falling Leaves Festival passed with Burk showing me the potions that turned people's hair temporarily purple and the sparkling animal phantoms that played with children.

I was waiting in line to get some apple pie when Anna came rushing over with Dryx following her with such ease that told me he would follow her anywhere.

"You could use a break!" Anna said, pulling me out of the pie line.

"But I want the pie," I said pouting.

"Dryx will bring us some. Just come sit with me," she said leading me away to a pile of square hay that people used as benches.

"Did he mention tonight's meet up?" she asked in a hushed tone.

"No and I don't want to talk about it now!" I hissed. I didn't want to think or worry about what would happen tonight with Rhein. I just wanted to enjoy the festival. I would worry about later, well, later.

Dryx came with three plates of apple pie and frowned at what I assumed was Anna and I staring at each other, but he said nothing as he handed us the plates. I took mine, deciding to banish any thought of coins and just enjoy the music as the sun began to set. I closed my eyes and breathed in the cool fall breeze, as I enjoyed each bite of the soft pie.

I opened up my soul and let in the magic around me. Paiza was a city of inventions and scientific gadgets, but the mountain simultaneously radiated magic. Together with the steam, the whole city was a blend of magnificent power.

"Emm, Tia," Anna poked my arm.

"Hmm?"

"I think those girls want to talk to you."

I looked at where Anna was pointing. Four girls almost the same age and height stood together. Two had the temporary purple hair, one with a darker shade than the others, but all of them had a star tattoo under their eyes.

I got off the haystack and walked toward them. Lowering myself to their height.

"Hello."

They barely whispered 'Hi' back and were hiding behind each other.

"Would you like to dance?" I said and offered my hand.

They giggled shyly and cutely. I waited until one of them took my hand and walked to the dance area, with the other girls trailing behind us like little ducklings.

I twirled with the girls, allowing the spirit of autumn to fill me with joy and hope. I was in Paiza. I had great friends. A new adventure with Rhein. Things were going to be alright.

Until it wasn't.

A hush fell over the market and I sobered up from all the celebration and dancing. My senses on high alert. Shadows crept over the buildings, exuding a stench of wrongness. Everyone was happy and dancing around me, including the little girls, but the voices were muffled. It was as if something sucked all the sound out of the air.

Dread filled me as I recognized that spell. *He was here.*

I looked around frantically. *Hex. Hex.* I wanted to release all my power, to hide everyone, but the moment my eyes fell on him, my body froze.

A man stood at the edge of the market, wearing dark robes that hid his slim body. His bleached white hair glimmered under the streetlamps that casted a shadow over his eyes.

Jaye, the Wielder of Sound and high member of the Court of Wizards was here.

CHAPTER 7

They have no claim on me.

My heart raced and I could feel my hands curling into fists. The audacity of them! Of course, they would leave me be until I was at the height of my happiness to make my suffering sweeter. Until I felt safe and let me guard down. And of course, Pari would send Jaye.

I opened my mouth, I wanted to scream, to tell him to get the hex out of my city, but no sound came out of me. He had trapped me in a soundless void.

They have no claim on me.

My throat closed.

Hexing bubbles. How did he pass through the walls?

Jaye disappeared through a door and the enchantment broke. Every possible sound around me rushed into my ears, overwhelming my senses and making me lose my balance. Someone tugged at my dress.

"Are you sick, miss?" one of the girls who was dancing around me said. Her oversized fake purple curls bounced around her worried face.

"I'm alright, sweetheart. I just need to sit," I said trying my best to smile.

I kept smiling at people as they greeted me on my way to the bakery Jaye had entered. No-one followed me inside and no wonder. I could sense the repelling spell drenching the place. The magical energy increased as I walked through the door. A small bell chimed.

Normally, the gadgets would be ticking and clicking as a metallic arm distributed the bread, while wheels moved slowly, showcasing the pastries of the day. But all was silent. Not one gadget was operating.

Sitting by the window, slouching with his legs crossed, was Jaye. A sly thin smile formed across his face. He nodded at the seat opposite his. I did as I was told and sat down.

"Living as a caller, I see. Amongst these trinkets diluted with magic. How degrading," he said, as he wrinkled his nose in disgust.

"What do you want?" I went straight to the point.

"Ah, witchling."

"Don't call me that!" I snapped, regretting it immediately as I saw the pleasure in his eyes.

"So testy," his nose wrinkled in delight, before he leaned forward, peering at me.

I crossed my arms and looked away. I hated how I could not defy him directly, even after escaping.

"You know exactly why I'm here," he said tapping his finger once on the table and leaning back, breaking his hypnotic gaze. My gaze fell on his wrist, looking for those evil strings of his and there they were like shimmering snakes wrapped around his forearm. They were very thin and very powerful strings. Every time I saw them, they were in a different color. Today, they were the exact shade of red and gold I was wearing. Jaye enjoyed torturing people with them. They stung like a hexing pixie bite. They were sharp and deep. Fear crept into my heart.

I won a battle against a *death* wielder, for bubble's sake. A sting shouldn't scare me. Jaye shouldn't scare me. I let my eyes drift back toward him, defying him. I could feel my soul curl up inside of me. I hated the level of power he had over me. Fear won over my defiance, and I moved my gaze to his hand.

"I am not going back," I said, putting my hand on the table, trying my best to keep my voice even. It was my choice to leave the Court of Wizards and it would be my choice to stay in Paiza.

"We've been watching you, witchling," he said, as if I said nothing.

I hated how he was good at making me feel small, but I stood my ground. He would not take me back. *Never.*

"I was very proud to see you stand up and fight that death wielder, all by yourself." His tone, his hexing tone, was as if he was talking to a child, which irritated me beyond control. "Though, it took you longer than I expected. I thought I taught you better than that." He shook his head, playing the act of a disappointed trainer.

"You taught me nothing of value."

"Ah, Pari said you were ungrateful." I winced at the mention of 'the Eagle', who was the leader of the high members, "But I assumed it was because he was such a boring man. I thought we were different. Closer. We had fun together, didn't we?"

"Fun? It was more torture than fun," I snapped. Heat rising in my cheesk. I wanted to blow this whole bakery up with him inside.

"And the ring?" he clicked his tongue, acting as if I said nothing. "You didn't even detect it when you arrived at this vulgar excuse of a city and I thought you were smarter than to fall for a truth serum." He reached for my hand, "I was heartbroken. Truly."

I swatted his hand away. It could be a mistake to anger him, but I enjoyed my moment of triumph. Though that moment didn't last as he snatched my wrist and hissed, leaning forward and pulling me closer to him.

"You think you have a choice in this, witchling, huh? You think you can leave us and parade your powers to those unworthy like it means nothing? You think we would allow you to soil our reputation by naming yourself a caller?"

I tried to pull my hand away, only for him to pull harder, his fingers digging deeper. My heart pounded harder as I felt the strings slithering on my skin.

"Yes, I have a choice," I said, gritting my teeth. *Bubbles! Courage, Tia, courage.* "You don't have a claim on me. Neither does the court. You can't force me to return."

Jaye dipped his head nodding, taking his hand off mine. Then the look he gave me brought me a new kind of fear, one that whispered that my worst nightmare was about to come true. He smiled as if he had already won this argument. In truth, he won before I even entered the bakery.

But, no! Hex, no! I gathered all the magic within me. I'd rather blow up this whole building than return with him. Perhaps it was better for me to battle him here and now away from the court and the rest of those horrid high members? I could feel the light ready to strike when a horrible mind-numbing pain surged all over my left arm. I bit my lips so hard, I tasted blood.

"You know, witchling," he leaned back, looking at the ceiling, returning to his *you don't exist* act, which for once, I was thankful for. He didn't notice how much pain I was in. My skin burned. I could feel sweat forming on the back of my neck. This wasn't him. He didn't hurt me. I somehow could tell the difference between Jaye's attack and my own stupid malfunctioning arm.

What is happening to me?

"For centuries, the court wanted to take control of Paiza. Its ancient magic should be under our authority and supervision, but the people of the mountain are," he waved his hand and squinted as if he wanted to find the correct word to describe them, "stubborn."

I blinked at him, trying to come out of the trance the sudden pain had put me in. I breathed slowly, realizing the pain had vanished again and as my mind cleared, something clicked inside of me. A possibility I should've thought of after the battle.

"The walls. You broke them," I whispered, barely catching my breath. Everything was making sense. How else would Thaiba find a death wielder? How else would they know of the ring?

He tittered evily, "The walls were never an issue. Yes, they are powerful, but not to us, not to the full force of the court. No, the mountain itself was hard to subdue. It has a spirit of its own. It needs to be willing to be linked to us. It's the kind of stupid sentiment the ancient magicians had. No-one would have been hurt by the wall breaking. The mountain would defend them. We just wanted to know how. It was just a test of power. That's why we sent the poor Thaibian army. But it all exceeded our expectations when you appeared and became the protector of the mountain in one very dramatic move."

"You mean …"

"Yes, my witchling. As its protector, your powers are linked to the mountain and your blood has been sealed at the court as a high member since the day we took you to the citadel. You are one of us and whatever is yours, is ours," he smirked. I was mortified.

"That's impossible," I whispered. My mind was unable to process everything he said. Was this another lie? What was real and what was a trick?

"Well, that is your problem dear Datia. You never understood the game of power." He pointed at the window, and I turned to follow his direction. "Yet, alas, you, whether you want it or not, are a part of it."

I gasped. The whole wall shined like a dome on top of the city in colors of purple, blue, yellow, green, red and black. The colors of the five high members intertwined with mine.

I sat there, confused, trying to understand what I was witnessing. My power was linked to them? My power was acting up? My power that was supposed to protect Paiza was now going to be its downfall?

"You have lost dear witchling, and I am here to claim our winnings."

"You can't have Paiza," I rasped, shaking as terror overtook me. I was the Protector of Paiza. *This was not happening.*

"Oh, no, we don't want Paiza anymore. We want you," he guffawed. "Say your goodbyes, my witchling. I shall be waiting outside the walls. You have *one* hour," he said raising his bony finger that sparked as the string clattered against his skin.

My arm stung again. I bit my lips to stifle a cry of pain.

He stood, leaned beside me and whispered, "You never had a choice."

The door chimed as he left.

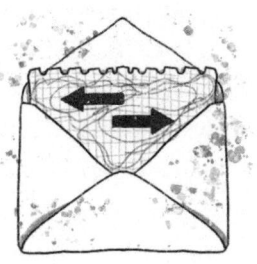

CHAPTER 8

Bound to the Court of Wizards. Forever.

I sat in the bakery alone, unable to make sense of what just happened. I looked out of the bakery's window. I watched as the people danced and enjoyed their time. How was it that a few moments ago, I was dancing with them, hopeful of the future, sure of my strength to fight whoever came my way?

Only to soon discover that I was never free to leave. What made it worse was that my magic was broken. I looked down at my arm. *My magic is broken!* And now I had to *leave*?! How could I leave this city? How could I leave my home?

An image flashed before me. The high members of the court owning this beautiful city, meddling in their rules and using the mountain's magic. What if they gave it to Thaiba just to spite me?

The realization hit me hard. How was I *this* stupid? I put Paiza at risk and broke my powers. I left these people helpless and open to an attack they could never repel. They would never stand a chance against the full force of the Court of Wizards. No matter how many inventions they developed. Especially if my powers were broken and bound to those spawns of evil.

It all dawned on me. My beautiful new life was crumbling around me. They were right. The members. All of them. *They were right.* How could I stay? It was all my fault. I was nothing, but a catastrophe. I thought I could be better. I thought I could do something else. I thought I was Paiza's protector. It turned out, I was its destroyer

Cursed pixies. Oh, what a disastrous hole I had dug myself into, yet again.

But I had to fix this. I *must* fix this. The wall was my mess. But how? I looked down at my left arm. Something was off with my magic. If I fixed it, perhaps I could unbind myself?

Perhaps... My hand brushed my forearm. A memory came to mind. It was a memory I hated. A memory of torturous nights before I learned how to control my wielding powers. The high members managed to wield it through inscriptions written all over my body with special ink. The memory I suppressed and wished I could forget forever was perhaps my salvation! Those runes inked all over me disappeared after each spell and I never knew what they stood for or how they worked. *If...* If I learned how to use them, I could channel my magic in the right way, without the fear of burning myself. Perhaps I could also find a spell or an artifact to untie myself from the other high members? I was the sixth high member and that was a new thing. There had only been five members for centuries. If it was a new thing, I could break it easily. *I think.*

Hex, I have to go back to the court.

It was a crazy plan, but a plan nonetheless. So with determination, I jumped off my seat and left through the chiming doors. I walked between the celebrating people, with one thought running through my mind; *find the gates.*

"Tia!"

Bubbles! Anna.

"Where are you going?" she asked.

The moment I saw her kind eyes, I wanted to fall in her arms. *Help.* I wanted to tell her. I wanted to confess everything. My magic, Jaye's visit and the mistakes I had made, but I stopped myself. This new plan was going to work. For her sake and everyone I loved in this city.

"By the mountain. Yes. You're going to meet him now!" she said, excitedly.

"Yes, yes. I am going to meet …" My throat was so dry.

Rhein. I was supposed to meet Rhein at the clock tower. We were supposed to watch the fireworks together. *Bubbles.*

"Alright! Go! And don't forget you are telling me everything tomorrow!" she said squeezing my arm. "Good luck!"

I just nodded, hoping I managed to smile before turning and rushing between the crowds. No-one could get involved. I had to do this alone.

I tried my best to politely brush away anyone who wished to talk or greet me and dashed into a dark alley. I reached a crossroad. The right would take me back to the castle and to my room. The left to the gates. I crouched on the ground, my whole body shaking. I wanted to vomit. The racing thoughts and possibilities rushing through my mind nauseated me. Was I making the right decision?

I had enough time to run and grab my things, but I couldn't make myself go there. Nothing I own here could ever belong to the court.

This was not fair. Why couldn't I be free? Why did my power have to break now? I scoffed. Wasn't this what I wanted? To not be so powerful? Oh, how foolish we can be sometimes, wishing and working for things, only to find out it wasn't the right thing for us, because we didn't know what we truly needed. This was not what I wanted, or did I? I didn't know anymore. I was more confused than ever.

All I knew was it was time for me to go. Today, Jaye managed to get inside the city, tomorrow the whole band of high members could storm in and claim me. There was no time for me to doubt this decision.

I stood and turned left.

Following the flickering signs that I was so grateful were still working, I reached the main gate. Through the guard's window, I saw a man in a soldier's uniform sleeping. A thought passed my mind. I banged at the window. The soldier jerked up.

He frowned at me, annoyed at this disturbance.

"The gates are closed," he said through the sound magnifying pipes.

I should have argued. that the gate was actually opened by a high member of the Court of Wizards and that he should be more alert, but I didn't have time for that.

"I need a pen and paper," I shouted through the window.

The soldier frowned, "I can hear you. You don't have to shout."

"Then give me what I asked for!" I said, still too loud for his liking.

He opened his mouth, probably to argue, but then a flicker of recognition passed his eyes. He figured out who I was and for once I was glad, I was the famous Protector of Paiza. He slid the window open and gave me what I asked for.

I took them with a thank you and started scribbling.

Dear Burk,

I am so sorry, but I have to go back to the court. I wish I could tell you about so many things, but I have no time and no choice.
Turns out, they do have a claim on me.
One day I will explain everything.

Take care of Rhein and Anna.

With love,
Tia

I pressed my lips together and tugged my curls as I felt the cool wetness of a single tear slide down my cheek.

"Please give this to the court's magician," I said to the guard, handing him my letter. He nodded, confused.

I took one last look at the city. Remembering every moment I lived in Paiza. I cherished these memories and saved every detail in a box in my mind. I would never forget the warmth, the happiness, nor the love this place brought me.

"I'll be back. I promise," I whispered against my better judgement.

I turned to the gate when I remembered something. "Oh," I took off my earrings and gave it to the guard. "Can you please give this to a castle maid, her name is Anna. She has long golden hair and a kind smile."

"Dryx's girl?" he frowned, taking the earrings.

"Yes, just give it to her and tell her... tell her, I'm sorry," I dashed away, pushing the small gate, leaving Paiza behind.

I walked down the green moor, feeling the spirit of the hopeful girl I was when I first laid my eyes on the walls I now leave behind. That girl was starting a new adventure. An adventure that ended with her returning to the place she escaped.

Maybe we do only have one destiny after all? I was a fool to think I could choose another.

Jaye, as promised, waited for me at the foot of the hill with a sly smile and a stretched hand.

I steadied my shaking limbs and I held my head high as I took Jaye's hand. I really *really* didn't want to go. But sometimes we must do things we don't want to get what we need.

A cold breeze rushed around us and within few moments, I was gone.

CHAPTER 9

I caught my breath as my feet hit new ground. The wind gushed around us, making my dress and curls flutter in a way that matched the agitation in my heart. The sun, still high in the sky, casted its light on the center of the Court of Wizards and its headquarters. We stood on a cliff, looking over the place I never thought I would see again.

Hexing bubbles. The High Citadel.

If Paiza was built through hundreds of years of inventions, the citadel must have taken millennia of magic. The pentagon shaped building was made of gray marble and it hovered over a gigantic deep hole where two crossing rivers met. Those ancient and roaring rivers sliced the court's land into four sectors and the fall of its strong rushing water rumbled the ground beneath our feet.

My limbs went rigid, as if a petrifying curse had been casted upon me. Bubbles. This was the last place I wanted to be.

"Easy, witchling or your heart will explode," Jaye hissed in my ear, relishing in my anguish.

I wished I could control the beating of my heart. I wished that panic didn't rush through my body, choking me. Because even through the deafening rumble of the waterfalls, Jaye could hear every sound my body made. I hated him and his venomous stupid power.

I tried to breathe slowly and steadily to calm my thunderous heart. *You can do this. Bubbles and cursed pixies, Tia. You can do this.*

We walked toward the edge of the cliff. Jaye twisted his hand. A loud crack sounded as a vine freed itself from a twisted branch and slithered toward us. The vine was part of an unknown ancient plant that covered the walls of the citadel. Unlike the moss that covered every building in Paiza, these vines were thick and dark. They were lifeless, like dried skeleton bones. They were used as a way into the hovering building. No-one, not even the high members of the court could magically transport into the ancient building, and so this form of transportation was created.

Jaye climbed onto the vine with all the grace of a charming elf. All dark and evil. I picked up my dress and climbed behind him. My cape got caught in a thorn and with a *slash,* the thorn tore it and tripped me. *Bubbles and cursed cauldrons!* I tugged at my cape, ripping it off whilst trying to balance myself on the dried vine, cursing the heels I was wearing.

Jaye laughed and I wished, I so wished that I could have slapped him right there, but somehow, I managed to compose myself. I stood there, my back to him, trying to breathe in and out in a calming rhythm, as the vine ascended and began its journey back to the court.

With the wind howling around us and the water rumbling beneath us, I prepared myself to meet the rest of the high members of the Court of Wizards. Those high members who could only live in this overzealous enchanted floating pentagon. It was a symbol of their power. A stronghold that showed, no matter who you are or how much magic you possessed; the court and its high members would always be above everyone.

The vine halted right in front of a massive metal door, one that was etched with thousands of runes. Unlike the ancient walls of Paiza, these runes had been crafted by wielders. It was started by the first group of high members and with every new generation of chosen ones, new layers of runes appeared. I was yet to mark the gates with my own runes. I scoffed at that thought. I didn't even know if I wanted to leave my mark on this place.

The magical gate sensed our arrival and creaked open. The rush of magic mixed with a mountain of memories crashed over my soul. Jaye walked inside. I hesitated.

I didn't have time to decide whether I wanted to enter or not, because a red string snapped around my wrist, as Jaye dragged me inside.

Hexing pixies. I will kill him.

I calmed myself; it was alright. I would just go straight to my room and compose myself. I promised myself I would be the definition of composure before meeting the high members, but of course they wouldn't offer me that kindness.

Four members in dark blue robes stood ahead of me in the entrance hall. The entrance, which was an empty square hall, was meant to intimidate the callers of the court and the rare visitors we received. The high ceiling was raised by four marble columns engraved with the same magic symbols as the gate. Murals of previous members performing magic covered the walls around us. On my right, the mural of Gally, Wielder of Fire, who manifested a whole city by enchanting lava. The vibrant orange and red radiated with the strength of his powers. Beside him was Sika, Wielder of Dreams, who stood above sleepers weaving enchanting dreams. The rest of the walls were covered with many other wielders displaying their magic.

"And so, the Wielder of Light finally returns from her *trip*," Pari rasped. He was the most dangerous wizard; the leader of the high members and Wielder of Shadows. His black eyes, which were slit by feather tattoos, pierced my soul, revealing every weakness. A shadow bird, an eagle that never left his side, stood on his shoulder, flexing its wings. Every nerve in me tightened with fear as everything came back to me. Flashes of nights when I was summoned for my powers to be used. Every time I was told I was a useless creature with wasted powers.

Next to him was Rham, the Wielder of Spirits, with his long hair that creepily covered his face and his heart tattoos. He was always the nicest. To his right was Cato, the oldest and the most disgusting. Teardrop tattoos decorated the Wielder of Water's face. Layers of wetness always covered his skin, whether that was due to his power or residue from all of the fish tanks he owned, I never knew. His moist lower lip had this cut that never healed. Saliva dripped from them. Disgusting. After him came Odell, the silent lean twig and the Wielder of Nature. He never said or did anything important. He always followed the rest and did as they did. Even though, it was said he had been the symbol of true power before Pari joined the court. Spineless coward. With Jaye by my side, I was once again in the presence of the high members of the Court of Wizards.

I forgot about the fear of being among them. I remembered its existence, but somehow my mind stuffed the true nature of that feeling into a box when I left for Paiza. But now the box had blasted open and all I wanted was to retreat and hide. Just hide.

Steady, breathe.
I'm alright. I'm safe.
I escaped. Cursed cauldron, I have escaped.
Why have I returned?

Hex.

Why did I think this was a good idea?

I wished I could say something clever or mutter a curse, just to wipe that disgusted look off Pari's face. But I said nothing. I did nothing. I was again the girl who thought she deserved nothing. The girl who brought nothing, but disaster and misfortune.

"You're back," Rham said with a weak smile. "I've missed you."

Rham was kind. He was always kind to me, and I knew he truly meant what he said. Somehow that was all I needed to hear to regain a bit of control over myself.

This was for Paiza. This was for my friends. *Rhein, Anna, Burk.* I repeated their names in my head, over and over like a mantra that helped the tension in my limbs ease.

Head high, child. Burk's voice whispered in my mind, as I lifted my chin up and tried a smile of mockery.

"Yes, I have returned," I said raising my chin. My voice slightly mousy, but I pushed through. "I am here to fulfil my role as an *equal* member of the court."

"Very well," Pari rasped, his lips twitching.

"Great! Let us begin then and be done with this already," Cato huffed with annoyance. Spit flayed from his droopy lips. "It's feeding time. My fishes are waiting for me."

Before I could understand what was going on, Pari snapped his fingers and a blue robe appeared from thin air, wrapping itself around my body. *What was happening? Begin what?* The members scattered around me forming a pentagon. Each stood on a corner with me in the center.

No, wait! I wanted to scream, but no voice came out of me. *Hexing Jaye!*

They hummed and wielded their powers. I could sense the ripples of their magic. Great powerful magic. I was paralyzed. I couldn't do anything. I tried to fight it, but the stars tattooed all over my body shined and burned my skin. I gritted my teeth. I wasn't going to give them the satisfaction of seeing me scream. Not yet anyway.

The humming increased and their tattoos shined, as a thread of light surged from each member, linking us together. It was as if heavy metallic chains were clasping around my soul. When the last point linked, the light dispersed around us and I felt numb.

"It is done. Her body is bound to the court's lands," Cato said brushing his hands together as if he just finished dusting an old cabinet.

"You can't leave us again," Rham said, cheerfully.

Jaye placed a hand on my shoulder and with a squeeze said, "This is your home, dear witchling. Whether you like it or not."

And they all left me standing there, shaking in the empty hall, as new glimmering bracelets of runes formed across my wrists.

CHAPTER 10

I stood in my old room, right in the middle of the high citadel. I was numb and cold. There was no turning back. Female callers in black hooded robes hovered around me, helping me undress, then dress. *Bound to the land.* It was bad enough that my power was already bound to them, now my body became bound to the land, meaning that I could *never* leave.

How many other spells need I overcome? What else were they planning for me? Have I doomed myself? I looked around, my eyes finding my red dress thrown on the floor beside me. My festival dress.

The Falling Leaves Festival. *Bubbles.* It felt like an eon ago.

I stared blankly at the windowless walls. One caller sat me in a chair. I could feel them unpin my hair. Curl after curl touched my shoulders. *Was it a mistake to return to court? Was I rash to think I could fix this? What was right and what was wrong?* Rusty cauldron! I didn't even know what to do anymore.

A caller stuffed my dress and shoes into a bag. I could tell they were going to throw them away and yet, I did nothing. I let them have everything. It was only when I saw the glint of the copper pin in the caller's hand that I moved.

"Not this," I said as I snatched it. Unconsciously, I held it to my heart. "Leave me be," I whispered and they froze in their place, "now," I added with more authority. I might be a prisoner, but I was still a high member.

One of the callers waved at the other one, before they all scurried away, taking everything else with them.

"Hex!" I whispered. The weight of my decision fell on me. I was here and I couldn't go back to Paiza. My lungs closed on themselves. I felt dizzy. I couldn't breathe.

My magic was broken. My magic was not strong enough for me to fight back and protect Paiza and everyone I loved there. My shaking fingers tightened its grip on the pin. I had to fix it. I was doing this for them.

Yet, my heart felt sliced open. I was sad, agitated and furious. I wanted to smash everything. I would've done it, but knowing that my powers wouldn't be able to return everything to its original state made me stop. I felt fury rising in my throat. This time fury at myself. Hex! I had to let all of these emotions out. Just once.

I hugged myself. I shouldn't wield. No, I was too afraid of that mysterious pain hitting me again and I didn't want to further damage my magic. I called instead. I called the air around me. *Please shield me.* A bubble of thick fog formed around me. One that muffled the outside world, a safe place for me to be.

I screamed a spine-chilling, piercing scream.

I hugged myself tighter. Blood trickled between my fingers from digging deep into the pin. I would take the pain. I would take the heartache. I would take it all.

I screamed and howled until my throat burned and I could scream no more. I took a deep breath, picked myself up and straightened my spine.

I will do this. I wiped my eyes, releasing the fog around me.

The first place I could check was the spell chamber, where I used to be taken. I placed the pin on a table, wiped my fingers on the night gown, smearing it with blood and headed to the door.

I took one step out of my room and a shadow slashed the wall before me. A dark smudge in the shape of a feather appeared where the shadow passed. Pari's way of telling me to stay put.

This act was meant to intimidate me, but by how dramatic it was, it reminded me of Burk and all his theatrical spells. That put a smile on my face. Instead of frightening me, that spell made me realize; *I can survive this.*

Today you win, Pari, but I am not giving up just yet. I stepped back inside, locking the door behind me.

***

The next day, the symbol outside my room had disappeared. Perhaps Pari thought I didn't need to be told twice or perhaps he was arranging other controlling methods? I didn't care. Whatever he was planning, I would worry about it later. Right now, the need to do something drove me out of my room and I thought since Pari's eyes were so fixated on me, I'd start somewhere safer and visit the spell chamber a few days later. And so, I stepped into the halls of the citadel, heading to its library.

There were rarely any windows in the citadel, which put a veil of gloom on the place. Small crystal spheres, filled with blue fire, floated on the walls across the halls and lit up the place in a very grim hue, adding to the gloominess of it all.

The whole building was made of gray marble. Even the doors. Everything was smooth and *gray*. The gray wasn't the light fog of Rhein's eyes, but the grayness of raging clouds. It brought a bang of nostalgia. I missed Rhein and his eyes. I missed my room and its big round window.

Focus! I told myself with a huff.

I passed hooded callers going about their daily tasks. They were responsible for the upkeep of the citadel magic. They made sure the blue lights decorating the walls were always lit; the food was always warm and on schedule, along with many other things. The stronger you are at calling, the better your task would be. The best task, of course, was being a magic apprentice to one of the high members. Wielders used to be the only ones who were allowed to be taken as apprentices, but there were not many wielders these days.

The callers didn't pay much attention to me, and I knew not one of them spied for the high members. No, their style was different. For example, right now I could feel the shadow of a bird following me. Probably reporting my every move to Pari. Again, I didn't care.

I was getting a book to read. No harm in that.

I entered the big hall of the library, which was only a few steps away from my room. It contained five high columns with rows of shelves carved around them. Each filled to the brim with hundreds of books. A mural of epic proportions covered all four walls. The wooden tables had matching chairs which were randomly scattered for anyone who wished to study or read a book. There was even a circle of cozy sofas around a big fire crystal. The library was meant to provide a comfortable haven for wielders to come and study their magic. But I never felt comfortable here.

That was due to the mural. The detailed image of lush green vines conjured around a powerful wielder was haunting. It was the image of Odell wrapping the vines around the citadel, as they became our vehicle between sectors of the citadel and vice-versa. I never knew *that* Odell. The one who was full of life and power. The Odell I knew was the weak puppet that Pari broke and used for his own will. I couldn't sit there, surrounded by the promise that one day I could be broken like that.

Bubbles. I shuddered.

I hurried to one of the columns, turning away from the mural. My hand brushed the books as I muttered their titles softly, ignoring the image of the wall of books back at the workshop and the bang in my heart. It was only my first day back at court, I reminded myself. I would miss Paiza less as time passed.

I frowned. That thought wasn't helpful at all.

I sighed as I choose a book, *The Basics of Wielding*. Bubbles; I was that desperate. I reached for it, when I heard a rattle as if chains were being dragged across the floor. I looked around, confused. I was alone. Just me, the books and the spooky mural.

Thinking that I might've imagined it, I went back to my shelf.

A cold breeze passed me, sending a shiver down my spine. I was wearing a simple dark blue cotton shirt and pants. A standard outfit made for the high members. There had been no female high member before me, so a dress was not an option here. Still, the outfit was comfortable and light. The weather inside the citadel was controlled and it was perfect. Not cold, nor hot. Just right.

I was about to pull out another book when I heard the rattling again and my teeth began to chatter.

"Alright, who's there?" I said, raising my voice.

The chains rattled twice and with it, I heard a soft laugh.

"Hex, Rham!" I called out, hearing him chuckle. "Show yourself."

Another breeze whooshed around me, bringing with it, hot air. I hugged my arm, feeling the new warmth as Rham materialized before me, from shadow to a solid.

"Hello," he grinned at me, propping his elbow onto his cane. Spirits danced on it, like a mirage of faces. Rham was the Wielder of Spirits, and within his wooden cane he held the power of an uncounted number of lost souls. They roamed inside the dark wooden stick in peace, waiting for his summons. Unlike the Death Wielder who practically kidnapped souls and held them against their will, the souls in Rham's cane chose to be with him. They were attracted to his kind heart and he had a way with them. A way of easing their pain.

I sighed as I looked at him. He appeared as usual, tired with his sunken eyes and thin cheeks. Yet, there was a glint in his eyes and I couldn't be mad at him for long.

"Please don't start scaring me again," I said, sternly. I really didn't want to worry about spirits visiting me at night, as had happened before. I bit my lips, ignoring the memory of Chi telling me how they called them *ghosts* back in Paiza.

"I wasn't scaring you. I was playing," Rham said, his face fell in a heartbreaking frown. "I told Pari I won't scare you anymore."

"And what did he say?" I shifted closer to him.

"Oh, he said you don't need scaring anymore," Rham said, as his smile resurfaced. To him, that was good news, but to me that meant only one thing. Pari knew the threat on Paiza was all he needed to gain total control over me.

I sighed and hugged the books in my hand. Rham leaned more into his cane and started to fade into his spirit form.

"Play with me," he whispered, as I rolled my eyes before deciding *'why the bubble not?'* I nodded and the ripple of happiness from him, made me smile. Rham was truly the kindest of them. Perhaps the only kind high member in this wretched citadel. His presence made me feel alright.

"I'm ready," he said in a floating whisper. This was our game. Rham would become a spirit and I had to guess where he was hiding by sensing him. Thankfully, my power wasn't that broken, so I managed to send my energy out to locate him.

"Make it harder," I said as I sensed him behind a column.

A chuckle was his response, and I could feel him drifting further away and cloaking his energy. I pushed more with my powers. I was edging closer to him when… *pop!*

A blue flame popped out of thin air and disappeared with another pop, leaving behind a scroll of paper floating in the air.

Rham immediately materialized in his true form and took the paper. He frowned as he read the content.

"Pari is summoning me," he frowned.

"You know, you can refuse his call or postpone it," I said, trying to tempt him to be defiant. If only.

Rham looked up from the paper with such a hopeful smile, it warmed my heart. He reached out with one hand to touch my cheek.

I stared into his eyes, pleading him to say no, just once, but his eyes said; *I can't*. Because as kind and fun as Rham was, he was also an addict. An addict to a magical herb that only existed within the court's herbal garden. Pari controlled its production and with it he controlled Rham.

"We'll play tomorrow," he whispered before dissolving into thin air.

CHAPTER 11

The following day passed with me hiding in my room, my nose in a book, focusing on finding any kind of instructions for that skin-inking spell. It was the only thing holding me together.

The two callers who were assigned to me came and went from my chamber, bringing me food and a fresh set of clothes. They made my bed, rekindled my blue fire and cleaned my room. *My room*, where I lived most of my life before I left for Paiza.

The room was the same as the day I walked out. The marble bed still hovered a few inches above the floor. The leather couch and its two matching chairs still perched before a blue fire that erupted from a marble bowl. The shelves remained held up by magic, decorating the windowless walls, but floated aimlessly. I used to have pots with colorful plants there, but I came back to find them dead. Of course, no one bothered to take care of them. Even Odell, who was supposed to love nature, didn't give them a second glance. I bet Pari ordered everyone not to do anything to my room.

I sighed as I sat on the only wooden thing in my room. The writing table and its matching chair. It was a bit old with chipped paint and rusty drawers, but it was the only thing in my room that made me feel like this room was mine. Perhaps because it wasn't here when I first came to the citadel. I got it from Odell who was throwing things from his room. I was around ten years old and didn't know how to use my powers well yet. I literally dragged it from the corridor in front of his room to my room. I was very proud of myself back then. That memory was one of the few fun days I had in this place.

My fingers brushed the rough aging wood. I smiled at the image of my room back in Paiza and I wondered what they were all doing. *Did they miss me?*

A thud snapped me out of reminiscing and I turned to find Jaye standing in the middle of my room. My high member robe thrown on the leather couch.

"You're required to attend our meetings, witchling. We didn't bring you back to wallow here like a pathetic caller," he said, playing with the strings on his wrist. Today, they were brown and ivory. He was irritated. *Good.*

My eyes fell on the pile of paper slips on the table. I had been having fire bulbs popping in my room all morning, delivering messages summoning me to my so-called duties. I had received that many messages, the fire singed a tiny circle on my table. I ignored each and every one of them.

"I don't want to attend any meeting. It's not like my opinion matters," I said waving my arm on the robe dismissively.

"Of course, it doesn't matter, but we require you to attend, and you shall do as we say," he sneered, snapping one of the strings against my pale cheek, turning it blood red.

"Hexing bubbles, Jaye. Fine!" I said swatting his string that still hovered above me.

He laughed as I got up and wore the stupid robe.

"Shouldn't you clean up first?" he said with a smirk, probably judging my ruffled hair.

"Why bother? I will only be around the lot of you. And I can't imagine how dirty I'm gonna be if I sat next to Cato. So, what's the point?" I said smiling as his irritation returned.

The string stung me again.

"You've lost. You could never defy all of us. The sooner you accept that, the easier life here will be for you. Now, go get cleaned and act like a wielder and a high member of the court."

"Or what?" I said rolling my eyes.

"Oh, my witchling," he said, taking a step toward me, his hand playing with my curls, "we could crush those precious shields you conjured up in that place you oh, so adore."

And by whatever look appeared on my face I could tell he knew he won, yet again.

"Fine," I said, pushing his hand off and throwing the robe to the ground. I snapped my fingers at the callers who stood in the corner.

I followed them to my washroom where a crystal tub awaited me. One caller summoned a stream of hot water that filled the place with mist. The other called for flower petals and scented oils that swirled around the water like a fairy dance.

"That's enough, thank you," I said, as they nodded and left me by myself in the foggy warmth. I took my clothes off and sat in the tub immersing myself into the warm rose water. This was probably the most luxurious bath I had ever had, but it wasn't the same. Nothing here was ever the same as Paiza.

Hexing cauldrons! I sniffed trying to hold back the tears. Sitting here would only take me to the breaking point I was desperately trying to avoid. So, I submerged myself once to get a quick wash and jumped up. I probably did that with a yelp but let us just say I was graceful about it.

I brushed my hair, wore a new set of high members clothes and left.

"Happy?" I spat at Jaye who annoyingly, was still waiting for me.

"And very powerful," he smirked, handing me the robe.

"Let's get this over with," I snapped, snatching the robe and departing without giving him another chance to mock me.

We walked toward the stairway. The noise of my sandals angrily tapping on the marble echoed throughout the halls. Jaye whistled, following me. He annoyed the bubble out of me. I reached the simple spiral staircase, which I never previously cared for. But now, after living in Burk's tower with its crooked stairs and wooden handles, I noticed how polished and shiny the marble steps and crystal handles were. Everything in the high citadel was aligned and perfect. Somehow, if felt very wrong and cold.

We climbed up.

The citadel had three floors. The rooms of the high members along with the library were on the second floor, while the first floor consisted of the kitchen, spell rooms and crystal dungeons. We were heading to the third floor where the council chamber was located, next to the training hall and other small offices that no one really used.

The third floor was as simple as the second. The walls were marked, either by a spell, or a mural dedicated to an old high member. or a mural dedicated to an old high member. The citadel didn't have any statues. They used to, but not anymore. It is said that a hundred years or so ago, a caller who was angry about something a wielder did, called upon the spirits of the statues and managed to inflict a lot of damage to the building. After that, statues were banned from the citadel. Even better. The place didn't need any additional opportunities for darkness.

I reached the council chamber and stood at the door, rolling my eyes at the sight of yet another wall mural. This one described the allegiance of the first five members of the Court of Wizards and their levitation spell that allowed the high citadel to hover above the deep pit for all eternity. Though, I've got to admit, it was one amazing spell. This mural was alright.

"Do I have to drag you everywhere?" Jaye said and grabbed my elbow. I just smirked at him as he escorted me into the vast hall with its thick marble columns and blue fire lanterns. A circular glass desk hovered in the middle of the room as a gigantic crystal ball floated at the center of the desk. Four high members sat on backless marble seats. Two seats were left for Jaye and I.

I sat down on my chair, not meeting anyone's eyes. I kept my gaze at the crystal. It was so huge, I could stretch my arm and reach it easily, touching the shades of white, pink and gray swimming across its rough surface. But I didn't. I had never tried to touch it before. The way it was a raw crystal, never carved nor polished, intimidated me. It was so real and the power residing in it was infinite.

"Let us begin," Cato, the oldest member, said and I shifted in my seat, trying to appear confident. *Head high.*

Rham, who looked thinner and more broken than usual, *the poor man*, tapped his cane twice and the crystal lit up. A moving image of a man appeared on its surface. The man was old with a white beard and had deep wrinkles around his eyes. He wore a formal dark suit, and his head was adorned by a golden crown, heavy with jewels. He blinked a couple of times then opened his mouth. His voice echoed through the hall.

"Greetings honored high members of the Court of Wizards. I am Tarren, King of Ladina and I send this message to beseech you to aid my kingdom. We have been plighted by a terrible disease. Our physicians could not understand its nature and have failed to find a cure. They inform me that it is not natural. I fear my land has been cursed and I seek your guidance and support."

Tears began to well up in the old man's eyes and my heart ached for him. His people must be dying.

"We offer you our allegiance and a third of our annual taxes," The King of Ladina continued.

"A third of their taxes?! They must be joking. That won't cover a quarter of the costs to treat his wretched people," Jaye said, annoyed, waving his hand at the crystal. The King's face disappeared.

The high members didn't argue with Jaye. They didn't frown or oppose his quick judgment. I didn't know why I was still shocked. They all possessed the same level of cruelty and greediness. They didn't even try to act like they cared. This was how they ran their business.

It was true that Ladina was a small kingdom on the edge of the southern lands with no natural resources or wealth, but that only meant they needed our help even more. They probably didn't have high-skilled callers. The thing was, the Court of Wizards created the laws that enforced all callers who wished to practice magic to apply for a license from the court. The court controlled the distribution of those callers and the best ones were dispatched to the bigger and richer lands. Wielding magic was more powerful than all callers combined, but wielders were very rare now. So rare that the only wielders alive today were around this table. That was why I was so important to them.

I clutched a part of my robe to try and stop my hand reaching for my curls. The members shouldn't notice any irritation from me. *Bubbling cauldron!* It was hard not to argue as Rham tapped his cane moving us from one message to the next. Jaye kept skipping the messages from those saying they couldn't pay the court enough.

I bit my lips, stopping a sigh as the final message manifested on the crystal. This time from a queen. She was the definition of grace with her white long hair falling over her light blue dress and her crystal-clear eyes. It was as if she was a living ice sculpture.

She opened her mouth and her speech radiated like a melody, "Court of Wizards, I, Calitha, Queen of Barma call upon your support to help us defeat the Vandums who dared to attack our borders. We require your best callers and battle enchantments immediately. Once we receive your support and the Vandums are vanquished, the court will not be in need of coal for five years."

"Finally! A place we can help," Jaye said with a sly smile.

Influencing the outcome of a war like they did with Thaiba was so obviously wrong, but I couldn't argue. If I was going to survive this place, I had to be patient and control my reactions.

"Then, let us agree," Cato snapped a finger and a tiny bright blue flame ignited from his fingers and floated before him, signaling his approval.

Jaye followed by wielding a similar fire to burn in yellow hue, Rham's burned red and of course, Pari's fire was the darkest shade of blue, almost black. The color of his shadows.

They all looked at me, waiting for my verdict. Cato raised an eyebrow and the corner of Jaye's lips twitched. Pari didn't pay me much attention, but I knew he was waiting too. This was a test of my obedience.

I remembered the farm and the attack on its water system. They were going to harm a kingdom just like they helped Thaiba attack Paiza. I mean, nobody even questioned the Ice Queen. She could be the one who was in the wrong here. This was so wrong. We shouldn't sell our magic to the highest bidder.

The table shook. *Hex.*

"Easy now. We don't want that temper of yours to ruin everything, do we?" Jaye said with a smirk. His thumb brushing the strings on his wrists. I could feel the threat in his voice.

Jaye was right. This was a game and in order for me to fix my magic and figure out a way to protect Paiza from them, I needed them to think they had won me over.

I lifted my hand, steadying it and letting it hover above my sphere. I took a deep breath and tried to calm. I focused and reached into my soul. Purple flames erupted on my side of the table.

Yes! My arm didn't sting. This meant I could do simple spells without my arm flaring up. I curled my hands into a fist before clapping.

"Good job, witchling," Jaye hissed.

I seriously wanted to punch him.

CHAPTER 12

Bubbles! Sleep!

I squeezed my eyes shut, willing myself to sleep, but I was wide awake. Thought after thought raced like pixies caught in a tornado in my mind. I listed spells that could break the binding runes on my wrists and other ones that could snap the other bond with the members. *Bubbles, they'd tied me up real good.* Between those thoughts, memories of Rhein kept slipping in.

My heart ached. It ached every day since I left, but nights were the hardest. There was nothing to do, but dwell on the endless possibilities. *Was Rhein angry with me for leaving so abruptly? Did he hate me for it?* Ah, the agony of it all. *Did he even care?*

"Hexing bubbling pixies," I grumbled, jumping out of bed, panting.

This was too much. I couldn't think anymore. I couldn't breathe. The walls were closing in. The windowlessness of this building was suffocating me.

"Hex this!" I whispered, before running out of my room, barefooted and slightly neurotic, searching for fresh air.

Reaching the stairway, I knew there was only one way for me to go and that was up. Up past the third floor until I reached a dead end. I lifted my gaze to the ceiling and smiled at the metal hatch. I reached for a glass handle and with an *umph!* I pulled it down.

A crisp breeze drifted down, filling my lungs with cool air. I sighed with joy and climbed up through the hatch and onto the roof. The vastness of the sky above and the land around me shot a chill down my spine.

I inhaled deeply. My feet froze on the cool marble, but I didn't mind. I was outside. Glimmering constellations danced across the endless night sky above me and the rivers hummed beneath me. I felt so tiny. I was just a dot in the middle of this floating box of marble.

Stepping toward the edge, I leaned onto a huge, dried vine. Flickering blue lights scattered around the land before me. It was the village sector, where residence of the court lived and where the market was. It was the only place that allowed outside visitors at the court. They were mainly those who wished to leave messages for the high members, or buy potions and spells. Through the years I lived at court, I had visited that sector maybe three or four times. I used to live in the sector on the other side of that river, the scholars sector. There, we lived as young prospective callers where we were taught about the ways of the court. I spent most of my childhood there until one night, I shined brightly as I slept. Purple light just erupted out of me, and I was sent directly to the citadel.

Bubbles, that memory was going to lead to gloomy thoughts. I turned away from the edge and there in the middle of the roof was the ritual altar. The altar was reserved for the most powerful and most dangerous spells. It had never been used while I lived at the high citadel. It was a carved pentagon and on top of each of its five points stood a tall crystal pole. I walked between them and marveled at the mosaic of symbols and incantations each pole was covered with. Each pole was special as it represented each member. At the top of those poles, the sigil of its owner was etched in black ink. I didn't have a pole to represent my magic. I was the heart. The center of the pentagon. I stood there, my toes tracing the five stars that were carved in the marble. I shivered and moved away from it.

I walked to my favorite place in the entire citadel. It was behind the pentagon where a gigantic oak tree settled. Its thick roots dug deep in the marble and its branches were dense with deep green leaves. Even without soil or water, the tree was green all year long. It shimmered with powerful energy. Sometimes I could swear I heard its leaves singing. It was made by magic, but no one knew how. One day, couple of decades ago, green light flashed from the roof and it just appeared there. It was probably a result of some kind of shenanigans the high members were doing, and it all blew up in their faces. Bubbles, I wish I had been there to see that.

There was a nook in its massive trunk. I climbed up, nestled into it and leaned into the tree's warmth. I closed my eyes letting the rustling of the leaves loll me to calmness. Warmth seeped into my heart, joined by a trickle of strength. No matter how many times the high members tried, they could never remove the tree. It was proof that surviving this place was possible.

I smiled, thinking perhaps I should sleep here…but then, I heard voices coming from the hatch. I pressed my body deeper into the nook to hide. I didn't want a caller finding me here. But as the voices became clearer, I realized it was Pari.

Frog warts! What was he doing here?

A familiar tapping sound echoed in the air indicating that Rham with his spirit staff was trailing behind him. I was far enough for them not to notice me, and the energy of the tree covered my magic. So, knowing I was safe, I peeked out the nook to see what they were doing.

Pari pointed at the center of the ritual alter and Rham, passing the crystal poles, went and kneeled on the carved stars. He placed the staff before him and leaned his head on it. His long black hair falling forward, covering his face. Pari stood before him and flicked his robe aside. Black runes covered his bare chest and arms. Those were the type of runes Pari used to ink on my skin, but unlike the runes he used on me, these were permanent and incredibly powerful. Those were the ones I needed to know how to use to help me control my magic. Bubbles, where did he learn that type of magic?

Pari raised a book before him and started reciting an incantation. I frowned. I didn't recognize the words. It wasn't the ancient language or the pre-ancient. It was something different. Something bad from the way he twisted his body reciting them. It was like his own magic was rejecting them. Rham, on the other hand, was ... shaking.

I remembered being forced to perform spells whilst frightened and I clasped my hand over my mouth to stifle a sob. I had to get out of there. But I couldn't move and even if I did, Pari would spot me. *Hex! Get it together!* I gripped the edge of the nook, trying to calm my shaking limbs.

I watched as shadow birds materialized around Pari. His voice became deeper with every word he uttered. Rham clutched his staff harder, and my heart ached for him. For all of his weaknesses, I admired his commitment. Even though this was probably in exchange for that drug of his. Still, my admiration for Rham made it a bit easier for me to watch.

That was until Pari muttered his final incantation that spawned the tornado of shadows which twice circled them before shooting into Rham's back, causing his body to snap into a backward arch. The wail his fragile body emitted shook me to my core. My heart trembled with terror.

Rham stayed in that arch pose, his hair falling back revealing red eyes. Not red irises, no, the full eye was red. Red veins ran from his cheeks down to his neck and his shirt was slowly burning.

Pari said something in his dark language and Rham, all demented, replied with a few words that sounded like a growl. I realized then, that Rham was possessed and not by his friendly loving spirits, no, something darker took hold of him. Something that shouldn't be awoken.

The conversation between Pari and the evil spirit continued for a few minutes. From the glare in Pari's eyes, to the twitchiness of the shadows around him, I could tell he wasn't getting what he needed from the spirit.

Pari lifted his book and recited another set of incantations. Rham relaxed, as the redness receded from his eyes. I relaxed. That was the end of it. He was probably sending the spirit back to whatever pit of darkness it came from.

But I was mistaken. A new layer of shadows swallowed Rham and left him kneeling, head bowed, on the cold marble. Green goo oozed from his body, as terrible energy pulsed from him. The air was caught in my throat and every nerve in me trembled.

This wasn't a spirit, but a darker existence. It felt like the end. Not death or darkness. It was just the end of everything. Fear was an understatement to what I felt when Rham opened his mouth and all that came out was a hiss.

I retreated in my nook. Hiding my face in my arms. Darkness swallowed me, one that was worse than the death bubble I was thrown into during the battle outside of Paiza. This brought a despair I never thought I could feel. The end was my friend. The end was where I belonged.

Then with a boom, the pulsating energy of that damned existence disappeared, along with all the dark thoughts in my head. I panted, laying on my back in the tree nook. My heartbeat elevated and my body was drenched in sweat.

What in the bubbling hex was that?

Pari's raised voice reached me and I peeked out again, only to find him snatching Rham's wooden staff from the ground and swinging it at him. Rham crouched down, his arms covering his face. And right then, I wasn't afraid anymore. I was angry.

"No!" I shouted, jumping out of my hiding spot and running toward them. My powers rumbled inside of me and somehow anchored by the tree's energy, a slash of light radiated from me. My arm throbbed, but the sting didn't come. With a wave, I thrust it onto Pari and sent him flying away from Rham, who was shaking and crying like a wounded animal lost in the rain.

Pari skidded onto the marble floor and with a flick of his wrist managed got to his feet with a graceful whirl.

"You!" he rasped in anger, peering at me through his short black hair. A shimmer moved across the ink covering his bare arms.

Bubbles! I did not think this through. But I couldn't stand by while he tortured Rham. No. I could do this. I could stand up to Pari. My magic was broken, but I had my calling skills and for some reason I could feel the tree telling me, *I am with you.*

Pari walked toward me, nostrils flaring and eyes blazing with a promise to end me. I curled my hands into fists and straightened my spine. If he was going to attack, I would take it proud and standing tall.

Just as I thought he was about to strike, something flickered in his eyes. He pulled back the shadows around us and formed the eagle on his shoulder. He reverted to his usual calm and cold state. That shift in behavior scared me even more.

He walked toward me, as a new cloud of shadows formed around him and before I could react, the cloud engulfed me. I threw myself at Rham, trying to protect him from whatever would happen. The shadows swallowed me whole and within a second released me.

I fell down on my back on what felt like a *rug?* I coughed and jumped to my feet, ready to call. But it was dark, too dark for me to understand where I was. I began to call for light, despite the whole place being lit with blue fire spheres. They glided around, revealing where I was.

My blood ran cold in my veins. Pari's workshop. *Hex! Hex!* I was in Pari's workshop. I looked around. Stacks of books and massive glass jars filled with decaying creatures were lined across the walls with locked dusty wooden boxes in the corners. Magic artifacts placed on various shelves hummed with magic. I leaned on a wide marble table, then panicked, because I realized there were no doors. *No bubbling doors!*

Before I could think or react, Pari materialized behind the table. I took a step back. He flicked his hand and a chair appeared behind me. I felt a strange compulsion to sit on the chair, so I obeyed, all the while keeping my eyes on Pari and reaching for my powers. I didn't care if the pain returned, or if I damaged my magic even more, I would not surrender without a fight.

Pari sat on the other chair opposite me across the table, his eagle resting on a dark stone above it. Pari also was wearing the high member daily outfit, like the one I was wearing, except that his shirt was sleeveless.

His feather tattooed eyes were set on me. *Who are you?* I wanted to ask. No one knew Pari's history. I didn't know where I came from exactly, but the day of my arrival had been documented by the court and everything I did after that was recorded in the main library in the scholar sector. Everyone had their past recorded, even the other high members, but not Pari.

He pulled a crystal from a drawer and placed it between us. The air around us was hushed, as a sense of dread filled my lungs. I had never been alone with Pari in a sealed chamber like this. And being alone with Pari made me realized something.

"Where's Rham?" I said, hating how shaky my sound sounded.

"In his room," Pari rasped. His voice was always like that, as if it came from a distance, as if casting spells in every language imaginable had effected him.

"And why am I here and not in my room?" I said, this time with a steadier voice.

"Rham had done his job. He served his duty. You on the other hand keep failing at doing so," he leaned back in his chair, waving his hand at the crystal.

Light shone from the crystal, projecting a blurred image.

"Somehow you never understood the value of your magic. You see, being a wielder is a privilege and a responsibility." The image cleared, showing a row of orange and apple trees. "Our powers separate us from those who are ordinary. It gives us control over life," he curled his hand and the row of trees immediately weathered and crumbled to ashes.

I was confused. Was this an intimidation? A show of power?

Then I saw it. Chi's face, shocked, running to the line of dark ashes. I gripped the chair. I wanted to jump at Pari, but I was stuck to my chair.

"What are you doing?" I shouted, gritting my teeth.

"Fulfilling my duty."

"As what?! A tyrant?!" I fumed at him.

"As leader of this court."

I scoffed and he thundered, shaking the whole room before standing up and releasing his shadows. A flicker of his hand saw the crystal show another image; fire erupting in the wheatfield.

"Stop it!" I shouted through the shadows. "You'll make them starve! Please stop!"

"Do you understand now?" he rasped, his shadows flapping around him.

"Yes, hex, yes. I'll do as you want." I said, as tears tumbled down my cheeks. "I'll fulfill my duties."

"As?" he said, his shadows receding, whilst the crop remained ablaze.

"As a wielder and a high member of the Court of Wizards!" I said looking at him, showing him through the tears that I understood his threats and I would listen. Bubbles, I really would! Just let them be!

"Good." He dropped his hand and the fire immediately ceased.

I caught my breath, my whole body shaking like a leaf.

"Don't worry. Soon, I will have my answer and I will deal with your worthless soul," he uttered with deep hatred. I didn't care. *The farm.* He attacked the farm! Just like that.

"You're dismissed," he said, and suddenly, I found myself in my room. Alone and shaking.

I fell to the floor and wept.

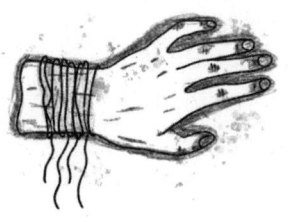

CHAPTER 13

"Did you *really* have to send ten flames to call me?" I said as I entered the sparring hall, waving a pile of letters he'd sent and I'd ignored. I wasn't in the mood to play Jaye's games. Not today.

"Well, if you came sooner, you wouldn't look like this," Jaye said, smirking, probably at the burned hole in my shirt and singed curl. My buffy eyes and tired demur didn't help my look either.

I huffed at him, exhaustedly, as he stood in the middle of the hall, wearing nothing but a black pair of pants. Thick black strings wrapped around his chest and forearms.

The hall we stood in was not impressive. It was just a wide, empty, gray room. What was impressive about it was the open wall to my left. The wall acted like a window looking over the cemetery. The notion of the dead being so close and the shimmering transparent wall that stopped the wind from knocking us onto our backs gave the hall an eerie feel. It was beautifully ominous.

What if I just ... jumped? Will the river take me? Or will these stupid bracelets on my wrist just fly me back up?

"Get your fighting gear on and let's start," he said, rubbing his hands together.

I only liked this hall for one thing and one thing only; it was the only place I was allowed to smack Jaye's pretentious face. He was a great magic fighter. The best from what I heard back in my school days, but I did relish the few injuries I managed to inflict on him. But that was before I went to Paiza. That was before I managed to scramble my powers into this uncontrolled mess. Before last night.

"I'm not in the mood to spar," I said crossing my arms. I had been avoiding coming here since I returned. How could I painlessly smack that stupid grin off his face if I couldn't perform any strong spells? This training wasn't part of *my duties*, so why risk it? That was why I could dare to ignore those nine summoning calls, but the tenth was particularly persuasive.

He eyed me from head to toe. Assessing me with his gaze that used to make me nervous, and eager to receive his approval. As much as I hate to admit it, not long ago, I craved his approval. But that need died inside me a long time ago, even before I left for Paiza.

Paiza. The image of the burned trees and crops flashed before my eyes and anger took hold of my soul. I stared back at him defiantly. Maybe this was my chance to irritate the bubble out of him without the danger of harming Paiza?

"Oh! Now you show the right spirit, witchling?" He laughed, throwing his arms wide open. My defiance apparently failing to annoy him. With a twist of his wrist, he whistled.

Out of nowhere, wind danced around me like a tornado. My silk pants turned to a dark shade of purple leather pants. A matching leather armor clasped tightly around my loose shirt. My sandals disappeared and I stood barefooted.

I reached for my powers as my eyes locked with Jaye's. *Come on. Let me take my anger out on him.* But something was very wrong with my powers. I could feel it confused and scrambled, like one of those mechanics back in Paiza when the steam ran out. 'On the fritz', they called them.

"I am not fighting you," I said breaking our eye contact and breaking the promise of a brawl with it. My power failed me. I could not do this. I turned and decided to leave. "I'm not fighting any of you anymore," I added exasperatedly as I pulled the massive door open.

A shrilling scream pierced through my ears and I fell to my knees.

"Hexing damned bubbles, Jaye!" I said, loud enough for my voice to echo through the hall. I managed to get up, ignoring the sting in my knees. "Your magic is the most annoying power ever!"

"Oh, I apologize. Was that too aggravating? Would you like a calmer voice, perhaps that of your beloved?" he said, walking toward me as fear trickled down my spine. I knew what was coming, and I couldn't stop it.

Jaye opened his mouth and the venomous words that spilled out of him were Rhein's voice.

Every inch of me shook with anger. "Stop it," I said almost in a whisper. My throat too dry. He kept speaking filth. "I *said* stop it." My voice got louder. I couldn't bear it any longer as he stood beside me, leaning down, his golden hair cascading over my neck and shoulder. He whispered, "Purple Hair."

A fire awoke within me. I screamed and I screamed, letting my power, with all of its wrongdoing, escape me. A loud bang threw Jaye off me and straight to the ceiling, leaving a web of cracked marble as he fell face first to the floor.

The pain surged in my left arm, but I didn't care as I dealt Jaye another blow. My anger was too great and stronger than any pain I could feel. One blow after the other and I only stopped when my lungs cried for a break. I felt like I wanted to cut my left arm off.

Leaning on his elbow, Jaye managed to prop himself up. His beautifully chiseled face was bleeding. But a wide smile peeked between the streaks of blood. He licked the blood slowly.

"Don't ever conjure his voice again," I seethed and before I could stop myself, I ran to him and kicked his face.

His hand shot up and caught my foot before I connected. He slammed me to the floor.

I gasped as the air was knocked out of me. I was shocked, and before I could react, he hastily slithered on top of me, pinning my arms above my head.

"Now this is more like it," he hissed, and I recoiled at the blood dripping on my face, my hair and neck.

"You are mad. I know you love whatever this is. This rush of controlling me stimulates you, but you will never control me. *Never!*" I spat at him.

"You can tell yourself whatever lie you wish or argue till your throat runs dry, witchling, but know this, you're bound to us now. There is no escaping this. It's better to accept it," he said before adding in the delicate fun voice of Anna, "keep everyone safe, yeah?"

I whimpered. I hated how much he enjoyed this. I was so hopeless. Yet, I could not give up. Not yet. Not after last night and not after he toyed with their voices like that.

I closed my eyes and reached out. I called for the land around me, for the wind and dried up vines. For anything that could help me, and I whispered, "*Rumina*."

Thunder rumbled through the hall, cutting my spell.

"*You dare to call in my presence. You filthy weakling!*" He roared as the echo of his voice and power rumbled through the hall, cracking every surface.

The wild look in his eyes filled me with terror. Terror I had never felt around him, because no matter how much he irritated me, annoyed me or even tortured me, this was the first time I knew he wanted to kill me.

And he would have, if not for a blue flame appearing above us., which dropped a letter next to my head. Whoever sent the letter, my guess was Pari, managed to calm the anger surging from Jaye. He let go of my hand and sat up, snatching the letter from the ground.

Even though, the risk of him killing me passed, the grin that spread across his face which reached his eyes, terrified me further. Whatever was in that letter was a more entertaining game to him than killing me.

"Well, witchling," he said brushing his hair back, as the cuts on his face healed, as his whole appearance reverted back to its normal regal self. "Your friend from Paiza is here and we should not keep him waiting."

He departed, leaving me panting and covered in blood on the rubble of the destroyed hall.

CHAPTER 14

I clasped my hands together, hiding them on my lap, under the table. They couldn't stop shaking. The official robes of the high members concealed the blood and dirt all over my clothes. I didn't heal as fast as Jaye, and I had no power left to clean myself up. I pressed my lips together. I had to appear emotionless. I could not react.

I sat on my chair at the council hall, an emotionless statue, even though my heart was a thunderous tremor. Music to Jaye's ears, I bet. Hex him.

My friend from Paiza. Who was it? Could it be Burk? It wasn't Rhein or they would say the King was here. He wouldn't come. I was sure of it. He had his people to think about. He couldn't risk it.

Please don't be Rhein.

The door cracked opened. I shifted in my seat.

It must be Burk. He would know how to deal with the high members. He *was* Paiza's court magician after all.

The tremor in my heart eased at the prospect of having an ally around, someone like Burk.

Head high and smile, child. I lifted my chin.

The doors opened and a man entered the hall.

He wasn't Burk, he wasn't Rhein, no he was ... Byron?!

Bubbles!

Byron was in a bright green three-piece suit that complemented his lean physic. His blue eyes and blond hair, now light again, brought color to the morbid hall. His chest was adorned with the official seal of Paiza, the three golden gears in a circle. His neck was cuffed by a swarm of metallic swirls, and I wondered if that was the choker necklace, he was so adamant to create.

"How marvelous are those trees? They just scooped me from the other side and flew me in," Byron said with his usual merry charm.

"State your business," Cato said, spraying the table with stinky spit.

"Well, greetings dear gentlemen," Byron said with a courteous bow, "and my lady," his smile widened as he saw me.

No-one returned his greeting, and the air felt colder. Byron swallowed and stood in a more serious pose.

"High members of the Court of Wizards, I am here on behalf of the King of Paiza, Rhein, son of Rylen and I request the return of Datia, our protector, to Paiza," Byron said, in a sense of authority I never sensed in him before. I felt proud of him, even though his demand was foolish.

Rusty Cauldron, Byron! What are you playing at?

"And why should we send our dear witchling to your city?" Jaye said, obviously amused.

"Her magic protects our walls. Surely you understand why she needs to return," Byron said with a flare of his hands.

"She is a wielder and a high member of the court. She can bloody well protect that city from here," Cato said thumping his sluggish hand on the marble.

"Yes, but –"

"Datia stays," Pari croaked, as I shuddered. Byron understood there was no arguing with that statement.

I curled my hands in a fist, the tension rising inside of me. They were discussing my fate like I wasn't right there. I wanted to argue, oh, how much I wanted to scream at Pari. But I stopped myself, digging my fingers deep into my palm and remembering Pari's threat. I wasn't going to explode. Playing it smart, I reminded myself of my commitment. I swallowed my voice and let them talk on my behalf.

"Well, we did assume you would reject our request. So, gentlemen, we have a business proposal." That got the members attention. Even Pari seemed interested. "You see the ancient Court of Wizards has had its eyes on our supply of magical steam for many years. You have negotiated collaborations many times with the previous kings, all to no avail. His Majesty, King Rhein, however, is willing to work with you, my esteemed gentlemen. We have to prepare an agreement between our courts and if I could be permitted, I will stay here at your citadel during those negotiations as an official emissary to facilitate the communication between the two parties. We have to, of course, discuss the amount of steam we are willing to relinquish, among other matters."

"And what does your king expect in return?" Pari said, stroking the shadow eagle propped on his arm.

"He demands the assurance that our protector will not be harmed and to allow her to visit our city," Byron said with a demanding tone. All the tension in me was washed by a familiar wave of warmth, one that comes only from friends. Yet, I couldn't let him do this. I couldn't let Rhein waste the steam on these people. Did Rhein really care that much?

"Harmed?" Jaye chuckled, "Did she tell you we're all evil here and tortured her? Curses, witchling, did you have to be so dramatic?"

I bit my lips. *Bubbles! Do not let him get to you.*

"Your proposal is agreeable, Emissary of Paiza," Pari said, his voice raspy and a bit joyful, which was not a good sign. He nodded once and out of nowhere two callers in their black robes flanked Byron. "Lord Byron shall be our guest. Show him to his chambers."

"Welcome to the Court of Wizards, Lord Byron," Jaye said with a snarky chuckle.

Byron bowed and turned, letting the callers escort him away.

As I watched him go, I felt a dark wave of energy directed at me. I shifted in my seat. Pari was looking at me. His thin lips curled in a twist. The shadow eagle expanded its wings.

I dreaded an attack, but it never came. Pari stood and left the hall, but not before his eyes told me that this new development moved him closer to whatever answer he was seeking.

I waited until the members departed the hall before I left, heading down the stairs to the guest quarters. We rarely had any guests as people were barely allowed to enter the pentagon, but I remembered exactly where those chambers were. I used to nap in one of them in the days Rham's spirits haunted me.

I walked through corridors, passing some callers. The high members were probably watching my every move, but I didn't care. The blood-curdling morning with Jaye and the shocking arrival of Byron, put me on edge. I couldn't deal with any additional unexpected surprises. I had to understand why Byron was here.

I hesitated for a moment as I reached the room, but then I knocked on the door. *Why the bubble not?* The door swung open.

"Tia, darling," Byron exclaimed and before I could say anything, he had his arms around me. His hug was brief and friendly, but he smelled of Paiza. He smelled of moss and metal. He smelled of *home*. It took all the remaining strength in me not to fall apart right then and there.

"Come in, come in," he said, ushering me inside. "I have to admit, as grim as those members were, they know how to live in style."

The room was quite identical to mine, as again, I was an unexpected addition to the original five, so I was given a guest room to call my own. Even though Byron had only been here for a few minutes, his things were already everywhere. His jacket was casually thrown on the leather sofa and the floor wasadorned with a with a dozen luggage trunks. Few were opened to reveal organized racks of suits and displays of metallic jewelry.

"Why are you here? Why is Rhein giving them the steam?" I said, angrier than I meant.

"Well, you didn't expect him to let them take you away? And so suddenly like that? I didn't even have the chance to tell you how marvelous you looked at the festival," Byron said, his spirit calm and happy as usual, which eased my panic.

"Is he mad at me?" I said, avoiding his eyes.

"He is heartbroken. Oh, darling, Tia. We have been so worried about you," Byron said taking my hands in his as a shadow fell over his face when he noticed the runes wrapped round my wrists like bracelets. Red bruises were forming on them. Bubbles! I forgot about that.

"What are they doing to you?" he said noticing my pain, the dark circles around my eyes, the slashes on my neck and the blood-stained cloths peeking from under the cloths.

"I'm fine, Byron," I said, taking a step back, away from his touch and prying eyes.

"You are obviously not, my dear Tia," he said, as his composure vanished. He turned to his trunks, trying to find something. "Rhein told me to stall before getting you out of there, but I think we should leave. Now!"

"No, no, Byron," I grabbed his arm and urged him to look at me. "I am alright, I swear and I ... I can't leave." I lifted my hand and nodded at the bracelet, "This is a very strong spell that binds me to the court. I can't leave."

"They'll keep harming you, or worse, *kill* you," he said, his fingers fiddling with a gadget he got from one of the trunks.

"They won't. They need me," I said, taking the gadget from him and putting it down. I held both of his hands and breathed. He followed my rhythm and calmed down.

"Rhein is right," I said, squeezing his hands, "You have to stall them. I am trying to figure out how to get out of here, and I bet Rhein is planning something as well. Do you know what it was?"

"No," Byron whispered, closing his eyes. I could see he realized he was over his head. Bubbles. I was too.

"You have to tell Rhein to stop the negotiations and leave me here," I said, hoping that he now understood how dangerous the court was.

"What?" Byron said, letting go of my hand. "We are not giving up. We can't let them take you."

"They didn't take me. I left on my own will. I didn't have any other choice."

"Because you left and took all the choices with you. We know that they must've threatened you. Burk told us a lot of the awful things they did in the past, or else why would you leave us?"

Their faith in me reignited my spirit. It lifted the darkness of this morning. But the images of the burned farm appeared before me.

"You don't understand. Ah, bubbles, I am such a fool, Byron," I said feeling the tears piling in my eyes. "I thought I protected the city, but by connecting myself to the mountain, I gave them access to it. They have access to all the magic. They don't need the steam or any negotiation. They already burned ... they already burned the farm last night, because ... because I didn't behave well... and now people will ... will starve."

"We know. Burk figured the situation out after you left and as for the farm, do not worry. We have plenty of food. No one will starve," Byron handed me a clean white handkerchief with a tiny copper gear stitched on it, as tears began to roll down my cheeks. "You didn't trust us enough to help you back then, but I am here now. Please trust us to do this. Together."

"Thank you," I said taking the handkerchief and trying my best to catch my breath through all the crying and sniffling.

"Don't worry. We will figure something out. Well, Rhein, Burk and probably Chi will. I'm here to be the messenger between the two courts and to be your friend."

I sniffed, speechlessly patting his hand.

"How did Jane react to this move?" I said, wiping the rest of the tears, trying to lighten the subject.

"Oh, my Janie... she let me call her Janie now," Byron said, happy as a puppy in the summer. "She is so proud of my new acquired status as an emissary."

"She is? That's amazing," I said mustering a smile. I knew Lady Jane was either teasing him or playing at something bigger. At least it made Byron radiate with love.

Being here with him, hearing about home, feeling their support and crying out all the pent-up emotions, made me feel lighter and a bit hopeful. We were all in this together and like he said, we would figure it out. Tears of gratitude formed in my eyes again.

"Oh, no, darling. Don't be sad. I come bearing gifts," he said with the widest smile as he hopped to one of his trunks. I leaned down next to him as he opened the leather trunk which had a golden gear stitched on its lid. It contained a variety of boxes, each more beautiful than the other.

"I like to keep my belongings organized," he said proudly to me as he rifled through the trunk, "now, which one was it ... hmm... no not that one ... oh, yes, here you go."

He pulled out a small golden box with a feather engraved on it. With a clink, he lifted the lid and took out ... letters.

A flutter rushed through my heart. Byron wasn't the only one here with me. More friends were reaching out, offering their support.

He handed the letters to me, and I took a deep breath, staring at them.

"What if they're mad at me? Or disappointed?" I said, my voice low and scared.

"No one from home would be mad at you, darling. Have a little faith in us," Byron said, as a cloud of warmness floated inside of me. He said home, like it was *my* home too.

He was right. I *should* have faith in them. Bubbles, when did Byron become so wise?

I took the letters and opened the first one. It was from Anna,

Dearest Tia,

HOW COULD YOU LEAVE?

I winced, but kept reading.

How are you? Are they treating you well? Burk assures me they will. I know he lies to ease my mind, and I can tell he is worried sick! I can see it in his eyes, and you know me, I don't trust outsiders. Especially the ones who kidnap my friend in the middle of a festival!

I am so thankful that Lord Byron agreed to visit you at the court and that he agreed to take this letter with him. I hope they allow you to read it and send a response. Oh, you better write back.

I can't get over how you were right there with me in the market and the next minute, you weren't. I am so agitated. Dryx has been so kind and supportive through these hard days. I told him I will not have our wedding until you are back. I can't prepare for the most important day of my life without my dearest friend. Who would make my dress now?

Please stay safe and don't disappear on me, alright? Remember, things are sometimes simpler than you think. Just say "What would Anna do?" and do it!

I assume you didn't go to your secret meeting with you know who? He is devastated. He fills his disappointment by working all the time. The joy you used to bring him is gone. One of the girls in charge of cleaning the rooms near his section heard the guards complain about how he hadn't slept since you disappeared.

I don't blame him. Everyone is on edge. Even the mountain.

Stay strong, my friend! We have a wedding to plan!
Love,
Anna

Hugging the letter, I was grateful Byron left to tidy up his stuff in the closet away from me. I didn't know how he would handle the new stream of tears rushing down my cheeks. Wiping them with his handkerchief, I opened the next letter. It had only one line.

Remember you are a powerful star, my child. Don't let them break you.

Burk.

It was all I needed to hear from him. There were no more letters. Nothing from Rhein. But it was alright. I was so close to giving up and was set on surrendering to Pari and his threats, but now I can work with Byron, let him stall whilst I found all the spells I needed to break me out of here and put my trust in Rhein and his amazing inventive mind.

"Thank you," I whispered, as I left.

CHAPTER 15

The days blended into each other. I spent my days mostly in the library or performing my duties, which were to go wherever Pari commanded me to be, such as attend council meetings. And Byron? I barely saw him. Only a glimpse here and there as he went to his negotiations with the members. I was not invited to those. I caught up with him in the corridors and gave him a shake of the head indicating I didn't find the spells I needed yet, but he always smiled and winked at me. We were not allowed to interact more than that as both our schedules were controlled by Pari.

I had to admit, not knowing what was going on with Byron and not finding anything useful in the library was stressing me the bubble out. Ah, the hexing evilness I was living under.

Suffocating in my room one night, on the edge of breaking down, I ran out into the hallway, feeling I should search for a way out of this hexing prison one more time.

I walked aimlessly between the empty corridors. Passing mural after mural, only stopping at a tiny drawing of a wielder singing. He was Alba, the Wielder of Words. It was said he could dry a whole lake or command a whole army, by just uttering a single word. He was a great singer as well. His songs were famous and people from all across the lands came to hear him sing. I wish I had lived during his time. It would be so lovely to have music played in the place.

And that wish led my mind to conjure a memory of mine. The music box Rhein sent me. The one I regrettably broke.

Rhein.

How could missing someone hurt not only the soul, but also the body? I ached the moment I left Paiza and I continued to ache every moment of every day. It was as if someone ripped me apart and left me broken to pieces, raw and hurt, waiting for me to slowly mend. And I was not mending whatsoever. Every day my pieces shattered to smaller pieces.

Oh, how much I needed Rhein's touch to comfort me, to tell me, *you're not broken Purple Hair, you can fix this.* I should've sent him a letter. There were so many things to say, but I didn't know where to begin.

As I walked around, deep in my gloominess, out of nowhere, a rich fragrant smell tickled my nose and cut my train of thought. I frowned and followed it. It led me to a metal door with tiny colorful gems tracing its border. It wasn't fully shut, and swirling smoke escaped through it carrying that smell with it.

Incense.

Rham's room. I knew his incense was nothing but trouble, so I turned to continue my search when I heard the loud luscious laugh of Byron.

Bubbles, what is he doing inside?

I prised the door open. Smoke danced around me, and I called for a cloud of clean air around my head. The last thing I needed was to be under the influence of Rham's mind-numbing herbs. Tempting as that might be given how stressed I was.

Rham's room was what I imagined the inside of a jewel would look like. The walls were covered with fragments of colorful glass and a rainbow of sashes and beads. A dark red carpet was spread out on the floor. Big cushions were scattered around between piles of dusty books, parchments and stacks of mirrors draped in colorful fabric. The whole place was a carnival of wonder that dazzled the mind. The herbal smoke however, blurred my vision. I felt suffocated. Hot too. I began to sweat.

Another laugh from Byron helped my eyes locate him between the clutter.

He was sitting on the floor, crossed legged and hands waving in the air as if he was telling some kind of adventurous story. He was wearing a shirt, his jacket discarded somewhere in the mess and not one single trace of metal was on him. He appeared so ordinary and young without his gadgets.

Rham sat opposite him with one hand on a bent knee. His hair covered most of his face, but I could glimpse a tiny smile that told me he was enjoying Byron's company. Between them sat a silver bowl topped with floating blue fire that burned Rham's concoction of herbs and fragments of incense.

"Tia, darling!" Byron basically shouted as I walked toward them to find him wide irised and beaming with a broad delirious smile.

"What are you guys doing here?" I said sitting down in their little circle. My posture was a bit stiff.

"Oh, sharing stories. Like ghosts and ships and stuff," Byron rambled. He was so out of it.

Rham craned his neck, allowing his hair to fall off his face. His face as usual, thin and waned with dark circles around his eyes.

"You don't have to fear the smoke," Rham said in his mellowed tone. I knew he meant to remove the protection, but I wasn't going to fall for that.

"My ghostly friend," Byron addressed Rham, "Tia is afraid of nothing. You should've seen her fight a whole army of Thaubis ... Thaifia ..." he broke off laughing. "Oh! And the dance. Tell him about the dance magic!"

I just stared at them. I couldn't figure out my move here. I didn't know if I had to have a move. Was this just an innocent meet-up between Byron and the only kind member in this hexing place?

"Tell him," Byron insisted, poking my arm and I swatted it away. He looked hurt, "You're not fun anymore. You know, you've lost your glow. You used to shine."

I would've felt offended or excused him for being under the smoke's influence, but he was right. I did feel less. As if the light inside of me was dimming. My soul was fading away with every day I spent in this horrid citadel, without a solution. Even Byron's arrival, which was a relief at first, had lost its effect with us being stuck in a rut. I was lost, digging an endless hole that kept on filling.

Oh, hex it. I pulled some cushions and I laid down on my back.

"Marvelous idea," Byron said. I could hear him shuffle, laying down next to me, as Rham silently settled on my other side.

We stared up. The ceiling glittered with colorful tiny gems on a dark granite. *Gorgeous.* I could lose my soul in that wide galaxy of stars, and I wouldn't mind it.

I could swear the gems were dancing above us. It was probably the smoke or perhaps a spell casted by Rham. I didn't care and time passed as we let ourselves drown in that magic.

"I need you to show me a spell," I suddenly had the courage to say. Rham turned to face me, with a mindless look on his face and a piece of my heart ached for him. I knew he was genuine whenever he complimented me, but the influence of these herbs and the control the other members had on him prevented him from doing anything to help me. But this was a simple request, and he wouldn't suspect why I needed it.

"When I was younger, Pari used to cast this spell on me to get my powers out. He would draw runes all over my skin. I need to learn how to do that. Can you teach me?"

"I can't," he simply said. He raised his hands and moved them as if he wanted to catch fireflies.

"Please Rham," I said, trying not to get frustrated, "I will play with you for an hour every day."

He smiled and I thought he was about to tell me, but his spiritless eyes gazed into mine before he uttered, "It's Pari's spell. He made it. He never shares his spells," which shattered my hopes.

"He used it on me too," he added with enjoyment like he was describing a fond childhood memory he shared with Pari.

I admit I used to be mad at Rham for not standing up for himself or helping me during those awful days, but now, seeing him in this raw fragile position, all I could see was how broken his spirit was. He was their slave. He didn't have any kind of control over his life. They stole that from him.

That realisation shook me to my core. What if that was my fate? What if I was destined to be broken too? Piece by piece, until nothing but a small fragment of myself was left? That's even if I was lucky. Fear seized me as I wondered; *what if I was broken to the point where I couldn't be whole again?*

"I'm sorry," I said to him.

That made him turn to face me.

"For how they broke you."

"You've seen death," he whispered.

"Yes," a chill made me shiver. I remembered.

"You got out. You're different," he said as the chill reached my heart. Why did he say it as if he was there? As if he was trapped in that cloud of death.

Another idea came to me and I said to Rham, "If I promised you that hour of play time, would you help me sneak out of the citadel and into the school sector?"

He closed his eyes and I thought I lost him to the smoke, before he was resurrected, whispering one word, "Yes."

***

"For bubble's sake, stop it you two!" I hissed at Rham who was levitating Byron who himself was hung in mid-air, laughing hysterically. "We need to be quiet."

The corridor we stood in was empty and it was late at night, but I didn't know who was heading our way or who was listening through the walls. It would've been wiser to try and sneak out on another day, when these mad men were sober, but I couldn't guarantee that Rham would have the same courage he was showing now. This was a chance I had to take, even with all its madness.

"He is so high," Rham giggled as he swayed Byron up to the ceiling.

"So blue," Byron said as he hugged a light orb. "I will make an earring out of you," he cooed at the sphere.

"You are both high," I huffed and grabbed Rham's staff. I tapped the ground twice and Byron hovered down and landed softly on the floor, still cradling the sphere. I snatched it from him and waved the staff at it. It floated awkwardly like an injured bird and returned to its place on the wall.

"Focus, you two. This is important!" I hissed, my nerves a tangle of mess. They both looked at me sheepishly. I felt bad snapping at them, but anyone could find us anytime.

"Now, Rham," I said, calming down and giving him his staff back, "Where is this secret door?"

"Behind you," Rham whispered.

I turned and there was nothing but a smooth gray wall. There were no magical symbols or runes to indicate a spell or any energy coming from it.

"Rham, please. I don't have time to play," I said sighing. I sat down next to Byron who whispered to the wall he leaned on. Something about Jane and a red dress she wore.

This was a rusty idea.

"I'm not playing," Rham whispered and held up his staff. "It's right here." He drew a shape on the wall with his staff then tapped it twice. A blue jewel emerged from the wall. I blinked at it. It was a doorknob. I flinched.

"How is that possible? I couldn't feel any magic?" I said to him, my eyes on the jewel.

"It's not a spell. I found this jewel many years ago in Agra. It can take you wherever you need. Just tell it," Rham said, his voice full of nostalgia and a bit of pain. My eyes turned to him. He was a powerful wielder and was once full of life too. He had adventures and memories. Now, he was nothing but a shell.

I refused to end up like him. I was not another Rham. I touched the jewel, whispered *the school library* and turned it.

A shimmering blue line emerged on the wall, cutting it in the shape of a door and with a thud, it opened.

"Take the jewel with you. It will bring you back. Remember the location of the door. We will be waiting here. You have four hours." Rham said, sober and serious. The first time I heard that tone from him, as if he was finally awake.

"Why four hours?"

"She can't stay for long."

"Who?" I asked with a jolt of fear, looking around.

"You," he whispered and before I could question him further, he took his staff and drew a line on me, from the top of my head down to my toes. His staff glowed and a spirit emerged from it. The spirit looked just like me. Same purple curly hair, same black eyes, same nose, and lips, everything.

She was me.

"She will hold the shadows away," Rham explained and my heart was going to explode with gratitude. "We will wait here."

"Thank you." I hugged him briefly before jumping through the door.

I gasped. Cold wind slapped my face as I landed on the ground. *Bubbles! I should've brought a cloak,* I thought, shivering.

Stuck in that temperature-controlled prison, I forgot autumn was here and the weather was getting colder every day. Yet, as cold as the wind was, my lungs expanded with the feel of fresh air and my soul was revived. There was something suffocating in that pentagon. Perhaps it was the continuous pulsating ancient magic or just the existence of those rotten bubbling members.

I didn't even realize how late it was, or I should say early, as dawn was here. The sky was a pale pink and birds, *real birds*, chirped as they flew above me, ready to begin the day.

A memory of Paiza's bright sky flashed in my mind with those mechanical birds zooming in and out of buildings, delivering letters and packages.

Focus! I rubbed my numb hands together and checked my surroundings. *Where am I?*

I stood in an alleyway between two stone buildings. One, I guessed, was the potion laboratory where new and old untested potions were tried and studied. I recognized its fortified windows. They were made with yellow glass. The toughest kind, in case an experiment went wrong and something exploded. The other, I remembered, was a windowless block of stone that I had never really ventured inside of, when I used to live here.

The scholar sector was basically designed as square blocks of buildings with narrow paths in between. It would've felt like a maze if I was an outsider, but I had lived here throughout my childhood. The details of this sector would always be seared in my memory. And so, without another thought, my feet led me through the paths. I had to hurry. It was too early for anyone to be in the library now, but in an hour or so, a flock of students would leave the dorms and head to their classes, scattering across the buildings.

Hex! I jumped here without the thought of a disguise or anything to hide my purple hair. Oh, and the tattoos. I tapped each one of them on my way to turn them into a shade similar to my skin.

Freezing from the cold and fearing that someone might see me, I quickened my pace. Two turns. One left, then right, I told myself. It would only take me a minute to reach the library, but it felt like eternity had passed before I saw its brown aging door.

I ran toward it and didn't stop when I got inside. I had to hide, catch my breath and plan where to start, because the library wasn't just a square building as it appeared from the outside. Oh, bubbles, no. It was a cave of floating shelves, unpredictable ladders, and enchanted books.

I hid behind an ancient ladder. One that I knew would be too old to move quickly, revealing my location. I was at the start of the cave where the usual books of the history of magic and basic herbology were located. For the books I wanted, the more advanced and ancient, I had to move deeper. I gathered my strength and walked again. Under the potion-making shelves and into a lower layer of the cave. The place was quiet, but it felt more hushed as I ventured deeper. I shivered when I reached the wielder magic section. The magic here felt different. The place was dark with the stench of ancient magic, but there was still something about it. A sense of pure energy. This was probably where I would find my answers.

Time passed as I scanned through the books. There was not much about magic illness or about depleting powers. I got two books about the higher arts of wielding, and another one about the strange tales of wielders. Maybe one of them broke their powers like I did?

Thinking I only had half an hour left, I decided to give up. Weaving my way back through the shelves, I felt discouraged. This trip was useless. And then, I sensed a sudden ripple.

It was a very familiar magic.

Oh, hexing bubbles.

I headed toward it. What was it doing here at the court?

I followed my senses and halted in front of shelves filled with books on herbs and mineral resources. My eyes trailed the shelves. There was nothing. I felt a tickle down my spine, another familiar surge of magic. I pushed a couple of books away and gasped.

The same exact black notebook I found in Burk's wall of books.

My heart raced at the memory of that spell and the image of the burning star.

I plucked it from its hiding place. I needed to destroy it. If anyone found it, it could lead to disaster. What if the members found it? *Bubbles!*

I hid it between the two books I had acquired and turned to leave, but my feet didn't move. A curious itch bugged me.

I wanted to check those pages and read that spell again. It was a bad idea, the worst probably, but I took a deep breath and snatched it out. I sunk down on the floor, my back leaning against the shelves and I opened it.

The mad scribblings were nowhere to be found. The lines, explanations and drawing were well organized and clear. Theories of mixing, calling and wielding magic and the original source of all powers were discussed on every page. It was packed with theories and spells to confirm or revoke them.

Then, I reached the last part of the notebook. The page that illustrated that spell I did. Unlike before, this spell required the wielder to draw an intertwined five-points star shape. Not the usual pentagon, but something new. The word *pentagram* was written under it.

"He fixed it," I whispered as I read the page again to make sure. *Hexing poison and rusty cauldrons. He fixed the spell.*

Like light finding its way through the shadow, an idea crept into the back of my mind. We are taught that wielders' magic is pure power. It came from within, and it was shaped into whatever we wielded it to be. What a scary thought that was. To have unlimited power. A silent power as well. No spells or rituals needed. No one can predict what would hit them until the wielder's attack is released.

But maybe that was a myth? An exaggeration? Maybe we do have limits? My magic was evidence. Were we really untouchable? If our powers were absolute, then how come mine broke?

And that revelation woke a fire within me. A fire that lit my soul ablaze. There was a way out and whether it would take me a year, a decade, or even a century, I was going to find it.

With this new energy I jumped up and left the library with my pile of books, heading back to the alleyway I came from.

I quickened my pace as I heard distant chattering. The sector was waking up. I reached for the jewel in my pocket and pressed it against the wall when I heard someone, a woman, call, "Datia!"

Bubbles, my hair!

I turned and gasped at the person standing at the turn of the alleyway. Three children stood around her.

"Meg?" I whispered, and before I could understand the encounter, the door opened, and wind swallowed me up.

CHAPTER 16

The rest of that day moved in a set of blurred moments. Dragging Rham and Byron, who were snoring when I landed back in the citadel, back to their rooms. Running to mine and hiding the books under my mattress. Pretending to be asleep, then pretending to wake up when my caller servants brought me breakfast. Sitting in a council meeting where the high members basically rejected every plea for help.

My mind didn't register the name of the cities or their problems. It didn't even pay attention to Jaye's attempts to irritate me. My mind focused on one thing and one thing only.

Meg.

It was only when the sun had set and my servants left me alone in my room with a tray of dinner, that I could finally untangle all the emotions that were growing in my heart like a spiderweb. I sat on my leather couch, ignoring my food, and staring at the dancing blue flames.

Meg, who I grew up with and who was my friend and dorm sister.

Meg, who I learned spells with and helped me make potions and explained hard enchantments to me.

Meg, who abandoned me when I was taken to the citadel.

I was shocked, confused, nostalgic, disappointed, betrayed, intrigued and so many unnamed emotions. *And the memories.* Bubbles, my childhood memories rushed through me as if seeing her, unlocked a door in my mind. A door that held everything that I was before I came to the citadel. Before I was discovered to be a wielder.

I jumped to my feet, the agitation driving me to move, to do something. *To go see her.*

I reached for the jewel that was still in my pocket. I was planning to give it back to Rham since I didn't know how he was hiding it inside the wall, but I could use it now. Just once. I walked to one of the empty walls in my room.

"Hex, just do it," I whispered to myself as I stuck the jewel on the smooth surface. My hand was shaking. It was time for me to turn the jewel but, oh, I didn't know where Meg was living. She was an adult now, not a student anymore. The dorms would not be it. From what I could recall she wore a teacher's robe, but those lived everywhere in the sector.

"Ah, bubbles, just take me to Meg," I said to the jewel and turned it like a knob.

The glimmering line appeared, and I clapped. It worked! As the door began to take shape, I realized something else.

Bubbles! This jewel could take me to Byron's room whenever I liked to know what was happening with the agreement. It was a key to so many things. But first, I thought as I opened the door and stepped into the wind, I have got to visit my past.

I stepped into a warm, faintly lit chamber. It was not like anything at court. It was *warm*. With a natural fire flickering softly inside a stony fireplace. Tiny pots were perched on the windowsill and were covered with flowers and lazy plants that crawled to the floor. Crystals and colorful rocks had been scattered across them, which reflected the flames like dancing stars. A trail of books had been left around, by the fireplace, under the window and on a small coffee table that led to one big pile of books of different sizes and colors by a big armchair that was engulfed by a fuzzy wool blanket.

This wasn't just a chamber, this was someone's home and it reminded me so much of Paiza.

Bubbles, my heart.

"High member," muttered that same voice. I turned to my left. It was Meg. She stood by a door, which I guessed led to her sleeping chamber. Her stance was calm, not at all shocked to find me suddenly appear in the middle of the night. She expected me, as if we had arranged an appointment to meet.

"Meg," I said in almost a whisper. *Bubbles, why was my heart beating so quickly?*

She looked the same and yet changed so much. Her raven black hair, which was always free and radiant, was now dull and pulled back in a bun. Her dark eyes, which used to always have a glint of ambition, were both weary and sharp at the same time. She was taller than me, always was, but she somehow now felt older.

"Would you like to have tea?" she said, pointing at the coffee table. The stack of books flew off the table, as two cups floated across with a warm teapot, ready to be poured. Her magic was fast and smooth. She used to be the best in our age group of students. She was even more brilliant than some of the older students.

"Yes, I would like some," I said, trying my best to mimic the maturity in her voice.

Meg nodded and whispered a few words. Two wooden chairs appeared next to the table. She picked up the kettle and sat, pointing at the chair opposite her. With another whispered spell the tea glided from inside the kettle and into the cups.

Burk would love that spell.

"What brought you down from the citadel, today?" she said handing me one of the cups.

"Err, I was looking for some books," I replied, awkwardly taking the cup.

"You could've asked one of the citadel callers. I'm sure they could've found what you needed," she said.

I recalled the many times she told me she wanted to be one of them. "I will send for you to visit," she used to tell me. My magic back then was so weak, I barely had a chance to find any kind of job in the market district. Being a citadel caller was an impossible wish.

I will send for you. Her voice echoed in my mind.

"I sent for you!" I blurted.

Meg looked down at her skirt, which was plain and brown. She smoothed it out, ignoring my outburst, so I continued.

"I sent for you and waited, day after day and you never came."

The fear of those first few days, feeling abandoned and alone in a cold dark place, rushed through me again. I had no-one and no-one came looking for me.

The cup shook in my hand. I was about to let it fall when Meg's hands reached for mine, steadying me.

Her eyes met mine, transmitting energy of safety and compassion, before muttering five words that shattered me to my core.

"They told us you'd died."

Those words were slow and heavy, as if they still carried the pain of hearing them all those years ago.

"What?!"

I retracted my hand, shocked, spilling the tea all over my pants and the floor.

Meg whispered another spell and the drops of tea soared from the floor and my clothes, before settling back into the cup, which she now took from me and set aside.

"Yes, they told us you had pixie pox and died," she said with a sigh, leaning back in her chair. "I didn't believe them. You were fine when we wished each other 'goodnight'. I asked around and looked for you, but there was no sign of your existence. I even tried summoning your soul, to no avail. Until…" she straightened up, serious, "two high members were visiting the market, while I was fetching some materials for an experiment. I wanted to take a glimpse of them. They rarely ever visited us common callers. Yet, there you were. Hair purple and grown, but it was you. I would recognize you anywhere. I was that happy, I wanted to scream. I wanted to run towards you and tell you I had finally found you, but then I noticed something. The tattoos on your face. My mind reminded me that high members were visiting. You were a high member. You went to the citadel and not me. You abandoned me."

"I didn't. I swear. I …" I started explaining when Meg held up her hand.

"I know you did. It took me years to understand, but I did eventually."

"How?"

"You see I always dreamed of becoming a citadel caller. It was the destiny everyone promised me I would have. You remember?"

I nodded.

"But my request was denied. Year after year, they rejected me and when I saw you that day at the market, I was furious. I thought," she averted her gaze from me, her hand reaching to one of the plants on the wall. She took a long breath before continuing, "I thought you told them to reject me."

"I would never!" I said, gasping. *But wasn't that what I thought as well? That she abandoned me too?* I reached for her hand.

"I know," she said patting my hand, "but back then, I was angry. I wanted, no, I *needed* to confront you. So, I snuck into the citadel."

I gasped again. "Hex, Meg. You could've been banished."

"I was too angry, resentful and worst of all, I was jealous. You, who didn't know how to enchant anything without my help was a high member. I couldn't bear it."

Her words should have stung me, but somehow in her weary eyes, I could see she didn't feel like that anymore. She was also right. I kept quiet and listened to the rest of her story.

"And so, I snuck into the citadel and looked for you. It wasn't easy and the more I walked around, the more I realized it was the worst idea I had ever had." She rubbed her neck, "I was such an idiot, letting my feelings get the better of me. But I kept looking and when I decided to give up and go back, I saw you and every bad emotion I had for you vanished. You were so drained of power, two callers had to carry you. Your whole skin was covered in black ink, and you were drenched in spells. I could still smell their foul odor. I saw you and I ran. I ran back to the kitchen and down the first vine back to school. I thought you had everything. I thought you left me here, but it was I who had left you."

"I had nothing," I whispered. I was stripped from every freedom and luxury, even from a friend like Meg. They scared her away. They scared everyone away from me. A teardrop fell down my cheek and Meg looked away, choking back her own tears. Remembering those days ached my heart, but hearing Meg describe me like that, made it real. It made every dark night I lived there real and that hurt more. It was like a sharp knife had re-opened my old wounds all over again. More tears fell down my cheek.

"Hex Meg! This is maddening." My hands shook in anger, "we have enough magic to help dozens of kingdoms. Haven't we been taught that the original five members established the Court of Wizards to help those in need and to deter magicians from using dark magic?"

"I guess," she began, conjuring a handkerchief and giving it to me. "Somehow along the passing years, greed plighted the court and and what began as a helpful tool, quickly became a game of fate. And now magic is suffering."

"What do you mean?"

"The members are depleting our resources. I'm working with a team to root out magic from the depth of the river's void. Why do you think the whole place is all gray? It's dying."

"What? Since when?"

"Since before we were born, but no one talks about it. And worst of all, anyone who fails, is banished to one of the wasteland cities."

"Bubbles! What about you?"

"I'm safe for now, but," a curve of a smile appeared on her lips. "Bubbles?"

"A new habit I developed," I smiled back.

"The old one though still persists I see." She pointed at my fingers intertwined with my hair. "You used to pull your locks whenever you couldn't do a spell or were stuck on a potion." She released a brief laugh.

I laughed nervously and dropped my hand. "How simple our lives were. Just worrying about a spell or potion, dreaming for simple things. Why are simple things hard to get?"

"Life takes what is simple and tangles it into a complicated matter. The test is how to untangle it," Meg said,

"I don't have the energy to untangle any hexing thing."

"But you do. You're so different from them. I might have been the clever one back at school, but you were the one who was full of wonder and adventure. I think I got the courage to sneak into the citadel because I knew that was what you would do and when I saw how they broke you, I was afraid, because I knew it would take a lot to break you. But I was wrong about one thing. I was wrong to assume you would stay broken."

Her words and the way hope crept into her eyes, pushing the worry away stirred the defiance in me again, but I was lost and confused. Would her hope last, if she learned that my magic was broken? I didn't know what I could do anymore or what I was capable of. The problem was bigger than me. The members were too strong. I couldn't breathe. It was too much, too overwhelming.

"I should go," I said standing up, grappling the jewel from my pocket, "I'll try to visit again." Before Meg could say anything, I pushed the jewel into the wall, whispered *my room* and stepped into the wind.

I managed to take one deep breath before hearing a chilling murmur…

"Welcome back, witchling."

CHAPTER 17

Jaye stood in the middle of my room. *Hex!* His hand in his blue pants' pocket and his eyes were wide and glowing with an evil hunger, like a snake who had found the fattest rat in the field. I wanted to run, but his strings were faster. One snatched the jewel from my hand and the other clasped around my wrist and pulled me toward him. I let the string take me. Fear had frozen my mind. How could I explain this or minimize whatever was coming my way? I didn't know.

He lifted the jewel to peer at it and the corner of his mouth lifted in a croaked smile.

"Beautiful," he whispered to the jewel before grabbing my hand when I reached his side. Twisting my wrist, he hissed in my ears, "Where could've you gotten this, little witchling?"

"I found it … in the library," I said gritting my teeth, trying to pull my hand, but Jaye's grip was too strong, and I didn't dare to give him more reason to hurt me, or worse, tell Pari. My heartbeat quickened with every passing moment.

"You found it? In the library? You just happened to find a traveling gem? One of the rarest magical artifacts in the history of this court? You just … found it?"

My lips pressed shut. I didn't say a word.

Jaye dropped my hand and I braced myself to whatever blow he was going to throw at me, but his lips twisted into a smile full of foul pleasure before saying, "We'll deal with this later. Now, Pari is waiting for us. He needs you for a spell."

My stomach lurched. *Bubbles, I don't need this right now.*

I wanted to refuse, to blast Jaye out of my room regardless of whatever pain my own power would inflict on me, but the glimmer in Jaye's eyes intensified as if he was waiting for just that, waiting for a reason to lash out at me. I bet Pari needed me awake and unharmed and ordered his loyal dog not to touch me. If I blasted him or tried to do anything, Jaye would have a reason to punish me. I could survive *that* punishment. Oh, he would make sure I was still conscious, but I refused to be dragged by Jaye to whatever spell they needed me for. So, I smiled.

"Happy to help in whatever Pari needs. I'm here to serve the court after all," I said, raising my chin. "Lead the way."

Jaye studied me for a moment, then chuckled. "You are finally beginning to get it," he said, pocketing the jewel and turning toward the door. I followed him.

We walked out of the room, down one of the staircases and stood by a spell chamber. I stifled a gasp. We had around a dozen or so spell chambers in this layer of the floating pentagon. They were all etched with runes and magical symbols, reinforced with crystal walls and magical artifacts to empower the high members to reach their maximum limits. They differed in purposes and sizes, but this one. *Bubbles.* This one was the worst.

It was one of the strongest spell chambers we had. The whole room was carved out of a huge river crystal. It had smooth walls that showed our reflections perfectly and a cold floor that gave me the sense I was walking on frozen silk. This room was carved and installed inside the pentagon by one of the greatest wielders. He was a builder, and he had all types of materials melted and shaped at his command. No runes or symbols were needed here as the crystal itself held a high amount of magical energy. I could feel it vibrating in the air.

The chamber was also the one where they had extracted a huge chunk of my power to store in the magical ring that ended up as a gift to the then Prince of Paiza, Rhein. It was also the room where my brown hair turned irreversibly purple.

The four members stood in their spots inside the chamber. Their barefeet finding the exact point of their pentagon corner, without any visible indication on the smooth floor. Jaye entered first, also barefoot, gracefully reaching his spot. I should've known this was where we were heading. Jaye rarely ever wore the standard blue pants and shirt, but this room required it. It required us to have nothing but our own powers. Even Rham couldn't bring his staff inside the chamber.

I took off my sandals and entered behind him, standing in the middle of their magical circle. I, too, knew my spot. I smiled at Rham who waved at me then my eyes met Pari's. He was standing between Cato and Odell. Without his shadows, and in this simple attire, he felt less intimidating. I noticed the tattoos on his arms that slithered up to his neck. An idea came to me.

"Perhaps it is better if you could ink me?" I said, "To focus my power better."

"Are you a child?" he rasped. His condescension and disgust dripped from him like venom, and I hated myself for having that idea.

"Obviously not," I said, more like whispered to myself as I averted my gaze from him. Well, that idea failed.

"Prepare," Pari commanded us. The shame and self-loathing manifested as a lump in my throat, but I swallowed it down. Hex, let's just be done with this.

Their powers were released, and I reached down to mine with a soft plea. *Please don't hurt me.* I felt the light inside of me rise as I let their powers guide mine. I didn't know what the spell was or who it was for, but I felt the requirement. A shield of protection and immunity.

My arm began to tingle.

The energy shifted. A blade of harm and vengeance.

My arm burned. I bit my lips.

An arrow of death and misery.

My fists clenched and I bit my lips harder, filling my mouth with the metallic taste of blood.

I could do this. I could bear this. *Bubbling hexing pixies.*

I breathed deeply. The spell intensified. It required many emotions and had many demands. The pain was too much. Spots filled my vision, and I closed my eyes shut.

My left leg! *Bubbles!* It started to sting. The pain was too much. I faltered. Almost fainting. I leaned forward and just before I slammed against the floor, a magical rope caught me.

It was Pari. His power slithered around me, anchoring me. My vision cleared and I could see black runes inking onto my skin. I tried to memorize the shapes and their representations, to try and find the source of the magic, but the pain was so bad, it blurred my mind. The ink though, soothed it. It gave me enough strength to tolerate the final layer of power infused in the spell.

When it was all done Pari lifted his arm and above me appeared a golden dagger that held everything the spell promised. It floated into Pari's hands and the moment he touched it, his power retreated, leaving me with nothing, but a soaring pain.

I fell to my knees, hitting the floor hard. I cried out loud.

"Such a waste," Pari rasped, and they all left me to my agony. Even Rham.

***

Somehow as the pain eased, I managed to pick myself up and walk to my room, shaken and weak. I didn't even bother to pick up my sandals on the way out of that wretched chamber. The callers would bring them later.

The climb up the stairs was pure agony. My left leg, *hex*, kept stinging whenever I moved my left foot. I passed one of the light spheres and I gasped at the sight of my left arm. Brown lines appeared all over my skin, from my fingers all the way up to my sleeve. It looked like my skin had been recovering from bad burns, leaving only these faint scars.

This was bad. This was really bad. If this brokenness that hit my arm moved to my legs, it would mean my whole body could face the same fate, the next time I helped with a spell.

"Hexing bubbles," I cursed under my breath as I finally reached my room. I never ever thought I'd be happy to see that gray slump of a room. I pushed myself to limp to the couch and flopped on the cold leather.

"Hex it, fire. Just start," I hissed at the empty bowl and fortunately, the blue fire listened to my command and erupted from the ashes.

I curled into a ball and waited for my body to stop shaking. I felt fragile and raw. A tear promised to fall, and I sniffed, stifling the waterworks. This was too much. Realizing that my magic was getting worse. The ink spell was a dead end, and Paiza was under threat by the members. Nothing was going as planned. Pari would rather die before sharing the secret of those runes with me. Well, he would rather kill me.

But he needed my magic, so he would keep me around, even if it was broken. It was probably better for him. I would not resist anything. Hex it, I already didn't want to resist. Maybe it was time for me to just give up? Give up on wanting more, on hoping to find a home where I belonged. At least I had a taste of that in Paiza. Maybe that was all I was allowed to have? Maybe I shouldn't resist this life anymore?

Sometimes, it's easier to just stay broken.

I closed my eyes, surrendering to the night and my dreary thoughts when I felt a ... buzz.

"Wh...?" Another buzz and I jumped up. Whatever that was, it came from the couch. I moved the cushions away and found a round copper disk. At first, I thought one of the high members was messing with me, but then I noticed the details. It was copper. It had a gear symbol on its surface. It was from Paiza.

I gasped and clasped a hand over my mouth. What did it mean? It was obviously a gadget, but what was it supposed to do? Is this from Byron? How did he get it to my room?

Bubbles, Byron. I owed him a hug.

I steadied my shaking hands and reached for it. It was a bit cold to touch, but I picked it up and brought it close to my heart. I sat on the floor by the fire, cross-legged and breathed in and out a few times to calm my nerves. Feeling I was ready to see whatever had been sent, I nodded to myself, looked at the disk and knowing how the gadgets normally worked, I tried to twist it, but it didn't work. There was no apparent button, but that was the only other option, so I kept pressing it, without result.

I huffed in frustration and placed it on the floor. I stared at it, my fingers on my temple. Perhaps if I called it, it would start? *Please, my dear disk, open for me.* Still, nothing.

"For hexing sake, just open the bubbles up!" I said, as the frustration ate any excitement in me.

Click. The excitement was back as the disk clicked before opening up like a blooming flower. I clapped. It worked! Me screaming at the gadget made it work. Oh, that made sense. They couldn't risk anybody opening it, so of course, they had to devise a way that only my voice could open it.

I reached for the blooming disk, still guessing what it was for when a ray of light projected onto the ceiling. I leaned back.

"What in the bubbles?" I said, a bit squeaky and loud.

"Purple ... Hair ..." A voice came from the light.

I sat up, stunned. My eyes focused on the light.

"Rhein?" I called, my heart pounding in my chest.

"Purple Hair, can you hear me?" his voice was so clear, as if he was truly here with me.

"Yes, Rhein, I can hear you," I said with a bit of a sob. The air barely found its way to my lungs. My heart was about to stop at the sight of him. Rhein. Right there, a bit distorted, but still there looking at me in the middle of the light.

"You're here," I said, rasping.

"I found my way to you," he said, smiling, as my heart cracked open at the sight of his eyes. I hadn't realized how much I'd missed him until I saw those eyes and every ounce of control I'd gathered from the moment I stepped out of Paiza disappeared. All the suppressed emotions and stored tears gushed out like a wrecking wave.

"Purple Hair, please. I didn't mean to upset you," Rhein said. I felt the concern in his voice. I shouldn't be crying right now.

For bubble's sake. Keep it together, Tia.

"Why?" I whispered, then sniffed, wiping the tear with my sleeve, before collecting myself, "Why are you here? Why did you send Byron?"

"You really thought you could disappear and I would do nothing? You thought I would leave you here with the people that hurt you the most?"

"It's too dangerous. They're threatening to take the city."

"You thought I would let them? Are we that powerless to you? Mountain's sake Tia, I waited for you in the tower for hours. I thought something bad happened to you. I thought you didn't want … Ah, you didn't think to tell me? Tell Burk at least if you didn't care for me? Didn't you think we deserved an explanation? You didn't even give us a chance to figure it out together. You just left. You left us. You left me."

Hearing it from him, like that, made me realize how foolish I'd been. I forgot that I wasn't alone anymore, and I didn't ask for help, but now I'd lost that.

"My magic is broken," I said out loud. For the first time, I said it. "I messed up. I shouldn't have left, but my magic somehow had started to attack me, and I didn't know what to do. I couldn't be the Protector of Paiza anymore and here they had this ink spell that I thought would help, but it turns out I can't even use that," I whimpered, "I messed up. I messed up bad, and now I don't know what to do."

"Purple Hair, you are as strong as any catastrophe coming your way. You can figure this out. We can figure this out."

"What if we can't fix my magic?"

"Then we will find another way. I don't care what we have to do, but I want you back. I *need* you back."

"I need to be back too," I whimpered. I was speechless. What was this never-ending, overwhelming day? "And I do care for you, a lot," I said, not meeting his eyes.

The smile on Rhein's face returned. "I miss you," he said, raising his hand.

"I miss you too," I said, reciprocating the gesture as our palms met at the edge of the light. My soul felt as if a cloud had descended and scooped me up to the skies. I let the light's warmth calm and steady me.

"We're coming for you," Rhein said. All the calmness I had gathered, instantaneously vanished.

"You can't come! They'll kill you."

"Don't worry. We have a plan."

"A plan?"

"Yes, and it has already begun."

"Right on schedule?" I couldn't help saying that.

"Yes, Purple Hair," Rhein coughed a laugh and everything inside of me crumbled into mush.

"And what does your plan say you should do right now?"

"Comfort you and ask you to please, trust us for once," he said with a stern royal face. "Did I succeed?" he added, bashfully, as he pushed his hair back.

"Oh, yes, Your Majesty," I said, giggling.

"You should rest," he said. His hand was about to reach for my face, *aiming for my eye tattoo I bet,* but he curled it back. Remembering we couldn't touch for real.

"I don't want you to leave yet."

"I can join you on the bed and wait for you to sleep."

"How?" I said, holding my stomach as I felt butterflies fluttering inside of me.

"Just place the gadget on the bed and I'll do the same."

"Alright," I said, feeling the warmth return to my heart. I picked up the disk and walking to my bed, before asking, "Can we talk again tomorrow? Is this how we can speak from now on?"

"Sadly no. It has enough magic for one transmission. I was waiting for you all night so I wouldn't miss this chance."

"I always keep you waiting," I said, my stomach now a knot of guilt as I placed it just like he said and laid down on the bed. The light followed me and there he was, right beside me.

"You're worth the wait," he said. I would kill Jaye to be able to go to Paiza and hug him so tight.

We just laid there in bed, silently. The quiet was nice and tranquil. Rhein was still a flickering image of light, but I didn't mind. He was there next to me, and I'd hold on to that as long as I could. Now that the initial shock of seeing him had left me, I managed to notice the stiffness in his jaw and the strain of tiredness under his eyes. I hated myself for causing him such pain. How could I have abandoned him in that tower?

"What did you want to tell me? In the clock tower?" I said, whispering.

He turned to face me and just simply said, "That I love you."

I used to wonder about love when I was younger, when I read the stories of old. The stories of maidens and brave soldiers, of witches and dark wanderers. I was curious. What did love feel like? Was it similar to the warmth in your belly when someone was kind to you or like when you're filled with bright pride after a teacher appraised your spell? Was it the joy you felt when laughing with a friend?

I never understood love until that moment. All at once, like a roaring tornado that turned my world upside down. That feeling was what I felt, too. I might not have understood it at the time, but I had felt it. It was the moment that our eyes met. The moment I lay my eyes on his gray ones, my heart had surrendered, and my fate was sealed. It didn't give us a choice. It was a tornado that turned into an intoxicating breeze filling me with shivers whenever his skin brushed mine. It wasn't just my love for this wonderful, kind and creative man, it was the love I felt for Paiza, my friends there and the life I was starting to build. It was the best kind of magic, one that transformed the world into a place that was happier and kinder. For that love, I would fight until the end.

"I love you too," I said, as sleep took a hold of me.

CHAPTER 18

"Wake up, high member." A soft voice said, as I opened my eyes.

A caller stood above me. I flinched. Her hood still too low for me to see her face, even lying down. The other caller stood by my bath chamber, all quiet and hidden.

"You slept all morning. You must wake up. We prepared you a bath," he said in a factual manner. Not demanding, not ordering and without a hint of kindness. It was just a fact. I overslept and that was not acceptable.

I overslept.

Rhein!

I sat up, my hand moving around the bed, under the cover, trying to locate the gadget. I didn't care what the caller thought of me. This would only confirm my weirdness to them.

"Bubbles!" I couldn't find it.

"High member, you must…"

"Yes, yes, I know. I am awake!" I snapped at the caller and regretted it immediately as she took a step back from my bed. It wasn't her fault that she was made to be like this.

"I'm sorry. I just …" That was when I saw a small, burned spot on my bed. Something singed the bedding, and I released a long breath. That clever king. The gadget was designed to destroy itself. I couldn't help but laugh. Now, the callers would for sure think I'm weird, but I didn't care.

The two callers fussed around me after my bath. Handing me my robes, tidying my hair, and performing maintenance magic, like replacing that bed sheet.

I stared at one of them who was conjuring a tray of breakfast. I thought about my conversation with Meg and how things were bad for the callers again. A bang of guilt hit my heart as these two had helped me with everything since I came back, and I had never paid any attention to them.

"What is your name?" I said as the caller placed the tray on my table. Both callers froze in their spots.

"We are your servants, high member," said the one, who was mending my bed and who always leads the other one.

"I know, but what is your name?" I said, turning to her.

"We are here to serve, high member," she repeated, but this time I could hear the quiver in her voice. She was scared.

I frowned at her, but then dropped it. "Of course," I said, not wanting to give them any more trouble.

How consumed was I with my own troubles that I had missed all the suffering around me? How blind was I to their pain? It made sense that the high members were mean to everyone, not only to me, like Meg had said, but I never considered it. I never considered Rham, these callers or the cities who suffered without our help. I was nothing, but selfish.

My mind went to Anna and all the fun days and laughs we had. I was a servant back in Paiza, but I was supported and loved. I was allowed to shine. I wasn't stripped of every right and individuality like these callers.

I was so angry, so irritated and finally for the first time in days I didn't feel pity or fear. I felt defiance. I needed to admit that my plan was going nowhere, and I needed to think of something new. Something to help Paiza, help all callers and help me get out of here, quickly. The longer I wasted searching for that stupid inked rune spell, the tighter my bond with the pentagon of horror got. There was only one option, I had to use that disastrous notebook again.

Bubbles!

***

"And some witch hazel extract, please," I said to my caller, who I had asked to bring me things all evening, as I sat in my room by the fire. I was faking making different potions.

"I need the practice," I said with a wide smile as I dumped a handful of sage into the bowl. Smoke erupted from the bowl and exploded in the room. I coughed and waved my hand, dispersing the cloud. The caller just nodded through a cough and left, happy to leave me to my madness.

I needed ingredients to test the new spell in that horror of a notebook developed by, who I assumed, was a mad wizard. From peeking into the notebook earlier, I realized it was the same one I'd used back in Paiza. The difference between both notebooks were the elements of the spell itself. Whoever this wizard was, he aimed to create a link to the origin of all our powers. The ancient magic that came before the rules of wielders and callers.

A *pentagram*. A whole new way of magic. I somehow wished I had known him.

I straightened and threw more sage, as the caller returned with the witch hazel. She just dropped it on the couch and scurried away.

Good. I stuffed the bottle into a sack I hid between the cushions and stared at my fake potion, waiting. The spell, from what I could read, was somehow stable unlike the old version, which was wild and uncontrollable. Still, I needed a safer space to test it. A place that was equipped with a powerful surge of power. That place was the stupid *hexing* spell chamber.

I tapped my finger on the warm leather of the couch and waited for time to pass. I didn't know the safest hour to venture out in, but I learned from my callers that Pari was not at the citadel and was not expected back tonight, so tonight was the best option. I still decided to wait. At least to make sure all the cleaning and preparation for tomorrow had finished.

When the spheres' blue light dimmed, I grabbed my sack and notebook and ventured out. Whenever the spheres dimmed, it meant that all work was done, and everyone was in their rooms. So, I rushed through the hallway of murals, down the staircase and stood in front of the crystal door. I placed a hand on it and whispered, *Allow me to enter. Allow me to use your magic.*

The door cracked open.

I stepped inside the hollow crystal. I was barefooted, not wanting to leave a trace behind me. Inside the chamber, I found my spot, right in the middle and kneeled. I hissed at the coldness that met my skin and pushed away any bad memories that promised to interrupt my focus.

I placed the sack in front of me and spread the ingredients on the floor. The herbs, the crystals, the witch hazel extract, the sage and of course, the notebook.

Bubbles, calm down. My heart beat with a mix of excitement and utter fear. This would either fix everything that was broken in my life or lead me to my death.

I opened the notebook and started reading. The spell was the same as before, but somehow the energy coming from the book felt calming and pure. *This will work!* I kept on reading, memorizing the steps and words. The blend of calling and wielding magic was more complex in this version and so I read it once, twice and a third time. When I felt somehow confident, I put the notebook down and began the ritual. This time it was smoother from my side, too. My hand swayed as if waiting to begin an elegant dance. After burning the sage, I dipped my fingers in the witch hazel and traced the intertwined lines of the pentagram, as I felt my power increase inside of me. This was right. This was true magic. Breathing slowly, trying not to get too excited, I calmed my nerves and traced the last line. And so, before me, hovering in mid-air, was the new shape of magic. A five-pointed star. Its center anchoring its core power. I sat there, filled with awe as I whispered the first words of the incantation.

A tremor shook the hall and I staggered forward through the pentagram, disturbing it.

Hex. What was that? Ah! Was I wrong? Was this too dangerous?

Bubbles, no! I am as strong as any catastrophe coming my way. I sat up again and clutched the notebook with both hands. *Rusty hexing cauldron, I will do this.*

I gathered my energy and whispered to the book, *please lend me your strength,* before drawing a new pentagram. I closed the final corner and adjusted my posture, about to mouth the incantation when suddenly I heard something.

Tapping noise. Sandals tapping on the marble noise.

Someone was coming. *Bubbles!*

Panicked, I shoved everything I had back in the sack and ran to the door, crouching behind it. Muffled voices echoed in the hallway. They were going to find me here. I squeezed the sack, trying to calm my panic. Maybe it was just a couple of callers who had to prepare the hall for a ritual. I could just make something up. But then I heard it.

The horrible chuckle of Cato. Then what was worse, *oh, bubble no*, the melodic voice of Jaye, saying something I couldn't hear.

My mind, paralyzed by fear, couldn't think of what to do or what to say if I was found. Worst of all, I couldn't let the notebook fall into their hands. That would be a catastrophe I could never handle.

"He is stubborn," Jaye said, his voice clear and close.

Please don't come here.

"He got us this far. You have to trust him," Cato replied, they were by the door.

Please, please. Oh, bubbles, please.

"I've trusted him long enough," Jaye said with an annoyance I had never heard from him, as they passed my door. *They passed my door!* They headed to the end of the corridor.

I clasped my hand over my mouth, stifling a sigh of relief.

Their voices trailed off to the end of the corridor and I took that chance to slip out of the chamber and run to my room before I noticed them standing at the end of the hall, with nothing around them.

What were they up too?

I hid behind the door again and peeked at them, my hands still clutching my sack.

Jaye whistled and the hallway shook as a crack cut the wall from the ceiling down to the floor. Both members disappeared through it.

It was a perfect opening for me to run back to my room, but all the panic and fear in me dissolved into curiosity. Where did that door lead and what were they hiding? Before I could convince myself otherwise, I ran to the crack, transporting my sack back to my room. My arm stung, but I didn't care. I was curious yes, but not stupid enough to risk taking the book with me.

Feeling lighter without the sack and fully determined to know what the hexing bubble they were doing, I stepped into the crack. The place was dark and made of stone. Raw uncut stone. I was met by spiral steps that led only down to a lower layer of the pentagon. I didn't know there was a level lower than the ritual dungeons.

Jaye and Cato's conversation trailed up to me, so I followed them. I stepped down the stairs carefully. It was too dark. I let my hand guide me as I squirmed at the wetness of the wall and the cold ground beneath my bare feet. What was this liquid dripping through the crannies in the stone? I reached for it with my power. *Water*. Was this under the river?

I hurried down the steps and a blue ball of light appeared through an opening at the bottom of the spiral.

"Just throw it in before I change my mind," I heard Cato's voice echo beyond the opening.

I hid in a dark corner and peeked inside what looked like a cave. A small dark cave that stank with foul energy. Shallow streams trickled from the ceiling and smelly fungi grew on every corner. The place was rotten. The cave itself was a normal forgotten cave. But what made it dark was ... a well. An ancient wooden well It didn't belong there, and it definitely wasn't normal.

Waves of darkness rippled from it, but it wasn't a threatening darkness. It felt like it was asleep.

Bubbles. Were they here to wake it up? I waited, focused.

Jaye and Cato stood opposite one another around the wooden well. Jaye was holding Rham's traveling jewel. "You will thank me once you feel this magic. It's a rarity," he smiled, his eyes hungry. He threw the jewel inside the well and whispered a word. To my utter shock, it was a calling spell.

The jewel vanished inside the well and I suppressed the ache of losing it as I watched what happened. A serpent of pure magic slithered out of the well and onto Jaye's arm, before entering his body through his nose and mouth. Black veins throbbed throughout his body, as his eyes turned pitched black. When the last sign of the serpent was consumed by his body, he returned to his white hair and dashing smiling self.

Cato, radiating with greed, leaned into the well and called his own serpent as well, and his consumption was uglier as his eyes oozed a green liquid.

What in the bubbles were they doing?

"The magic is getting weaker. The last supply wasn't as good as we expected. If I hadn't have found this by accident, we'd have been screwed!" Jaye growled. Few black vines throbbed around his twisted mouth. "We need the mountain's magic."

"Pari says ..."

"Hex Pari. He is obsessed with his stupid spell. How many times does he need to fail to admit it? He can't extract pure wielders powers. Remember what happened with Odell?"

"Datia is different. Weaker. He can steal her powers."

"He is just obsessed with her. That girl's powers are useless. The mountain is better. Paiza is stronger and easier. It's there for us to take."

"We can't defy him, Jaye. We owe him everything."

"We owe him nothing! It's true he shared the well with us and turned us into wielders, but we have more than repaid him throughout the years. He has one chance," Jaye said, his golden eyes crackling with powers, "if he can't extract Datia's magic *soon*, I'm heading to that mountain."

Their argument kept going round in circles, but I couldn't listen anymore. What I heard was enough.

The magic is weaker ... The last supply ... Pure wielders .... Steal her powers.

Bubbles!

I ran.

CHAPTER 19

They were stealing powers. They were not real wielders. *How? How was this possible? Was I like them too? Did they give me this power? Is that why it broke? Because I stayed away from the court for too long?* No, it couldn't be. He said Pari wanted to steal my power. My magic was real.

Bubbles, I'm so confused!

Disoriented and out of breath, I sank down to my knees in the hallway. Hex, I didn't even know what hallway or which level I was in. My mind was a hazy blur. I buried my head in my hands and just tried to understand what had just happened.

Alright. Focus. I saw Jaye and Cato summon and enter a secret door that somehow took us to a cave. That door, the crack in the wall, was probably a magical portal that transported us under the river. Jaye threw the traveling jewel into the well and somehow the well, which reeked with dark magic, had in some way stripped the jewel of its powers, and Jaye and Cato *absorbed* it? And they wanted to do the same to the mountain of Paiza. To *me*? They wanted to throw me into the well and absorb *me*?

I whimpered. I was so dead. Coming back was a mistake. I had to leave. Now!

I stood up and ran again. This time to Rham's room. I entered through the bejeweled door and searched for Rham's sleeping body through his mess.

"Rham," I whispered through all the trinkets. I couldn't find him.

"Here," a faint woman's voice said, which caused me to flinch as I saw the gray spirit of a young woman with long black hair and a horrible wound on her chest, float atop a pile of blankets.

"Thank you," I whispered as I peeled the blanket off, finding Rham fast asleep.

"Rham, wake up." I shook him awake.

"Is it time for a spell?" he slurred.

"Yes, yes, it is."

"Datia?" he blinked at me.

"I need you to conjure that copy of me again," I said urgently helping him sit up.

"Why? What is happening?" he looked at me extremely confused.

"I have somewhere to go to. Can you transfer my bond to her?"

"You are leaving us?" his eyes looked too hurt it broke my heart. "You can't. Not again."

"It's just for a day. I promise. I will come back," I said in a slow kind way, like I was promising a child a treat.

He looked around, not sure of what to do. I took his face in my hands.

"Please Rham. I need this."

His hands reached up to my face and we stared at each other for a moment. Then he nodded.

I released him and he found his staff before tapping it three times. My exact replica materialized. Just like before, but this time, she had my bracelet of runes.

I looked down at my own wrists and smiled at my clear skin.

"Thank you!" I said to Rham and kissed his cheek. "I will come back for you."

Somehow, someday, I told myself, *I would keep that promise.*

And with that, I ran again. This time to Byron. I reached his room and banged on his door.

He opened the door, eyes buffy and hair ruffled. He was wearing a silk shirt, pants and a fabric eye cover wrapped around his neck.

"Tia?" he said, alarmed by my panicked appearance. "Darling, what is the matter?"

"Things are worse than I thought," I said, feeling the weight of my discovery and everything I had been through in this cursed place crashing around me.

"Come in," he pulled me in and locked the door behind me. "What is happening?"

"They want to kill me!" I snapped, frantically. I felt my body burning with panic. Sweat trickling down my back. I brushed back my hair and spelled it into a bun. I needed water. I saw a water jug by Byron's bed and ran to it. I drank and drank, water spilling down onto my clothes, but I didn't care.

"Oh. That was one of the possibilities I was told about," he said as the color drained from his face.

"We need to leave," I said, waving the jug, splattering the water all over the place. "Now!"

"What about your bond thingy," he said raising his wrists to me.

"I've managed to momentarily pause it," I said as I threw the jug onto the bed. Somehow the water cooled me down and my mind was clearing up. "But we don't have much time."

"Oh dear," he frowned, before suddenly clapping once. His eyes became full of determination. "Fear not! Rhein told me we might need to sneak you out, but I never thought we could use it with that ugly bracelet of yours," Byron said walking to his trunks. His room was messier than when I saw it the first day he arrived at the court. Shirts and accessories and gadgets were scattered everywhere. I expected Byron to be neater,

I had Byron. I had Rhein. I had Burk. I had Anna. I had all of Paiza. I tried to calm myself. I was getting out of here.

"It's quite risky and it was only meant to be used as a last resort," Byron said as he emptied one of his trunks, "but since you might be killed soon, I believe it's the appropriate time."

Byron nodded when the trunk was empty. He then pressed the screws on each side. The trunk clicked and whirled for a few moments before it unfurled into a tall arched copper frame, but it was empty. Byron knelt by it and again fidgeted with it, pressing buttons and twisting the gear at the bottom of the frame. That was when I noticed the small engine inside the frame's base. My hands reached for my chest. Rhein's engine. Ah, my heart could not take the waves of different emotions that had spent the last day rushing through my body! Ah, bubbles! I just wanted to go to Paiza. Broken magic or not. I didn't care anymore. I wanted to leave.

"Step back," Byron said, jumping to his feet. We both stood away from the frame that now buzzed with power.

"It will need a minute to charge up and then we can step through it and go home," Byron said and I couldn't breathe.

Home. I smiled. *I was going home.* I held Byron's hand.

We watched as a bright white light, the same that erupted from the gadget I used yesterday, started to manifest from the base. It rose slowly to fill the frame with crackling whiteness. I squeezed Byron's hand and my heart filled with elation as I noticed an image forming in the light.

I took a step forward, but Byron pulled me back.

"The light has to fill the frame completely. See the glass ball on the top?" he said pointing at the frame. "It has to shine, then we will be able to walk through it."

I nodded. *Please. Please work.*

The light reached the top and I impatiently rose with it, standing on my tiptoes. I wanted to pass through it. My eyes stared at the ball, waiting for it to shine, to give me the signal that I was going back to my true home.

The image through the light cleared and my soul felt alive at the sight of Rhein's chamber. I could recognize it anywhere. And he was there, standing by a table talking to someone I couldn't recognize.

"Rhein!" I called at the frame, and he turned. He blinked at us, smiled widely before his face darkened. He frowned, shaking his head, mouthing something we couldn't hear.

Just when we were about to step in, the frame exploded with a loud bang and I screamed as my body slammed against the floor, knocking the breath out of me. My mind buzzed with the echo of the blast and my vision was hazy. The whole room was covered with soot and dust.

"Byron!" I shouted, trying to locate him amidst a coughing fit.

I waved off the cloud of dust only to find the gadget, the one that would take me back to Paiza, broken to pieces. *No!* And behind it, a body laid on the floor. *Byron.* His face slashed and smeared with blood.

I stood, ignoring the ache that was spreading all over me. I had to make sure Byron was alive and well. I took two steps before shadows erupted from everywhere. The floor, the ceiling, the wall. Everywhere. They twisted and swirled all over us, only to gather in the middle, right on top of the broken pieces of copper. The shadows dispersed, revealing a furious Pari standing between an annoyed Cato and a very happy Jaye. Rham cowered behind Pari. His eyes sad and apologetic. Hex him! He told them.

"Naughty witchling," Jaye said, smiling like someone who'd found a pot of gold.

"Enough!" Pari rasped, snapping his fingers. "It's time to get rid of you!"

"Ah!" I screamed as ropes of shadow forced my hand behind my back and tied it up. Similar ropes tied Byron's hands and feet.

"You liars. You thieves!" I hissed at them, my blood boiling with rage. "You call yourselves wielders?! You shamed the rest for being callers?! At least they live honorably! Unlike you! You ... you leeches! Sucking the powers of those who are stronger than you!"

"Silence her," Pari ordered Jaye.

"My pleasure," Jaye smirked and whistled.

It was as if a cord had ripped inside my throat. I opened my mouth to cry, but no sound came out. My pounding, thunderous heart was the only sound emerging from me. I reached for my powers, furious. I didn't care if I died after this. No one took my voice or my freedom like this. But alas, I couldn't feel anything. I squeezed my eyes shut, focusing. *Come on, magic. Please help me.* But nothing.

"Don't try and fight. Your power is mine now," Pari growled, smiling wide for the first time. It wasn't a normal happy smile, not the wicked ones of Jaye. No, this was a smile of madness, lips spreading wide and eyes bulging. He lifted his hand to reveal a new ink drawn on his palm. A twisted letter. It felt foul, like the well in that cave. And it all clicked. Jaye said that Pari tried to steal a wielder's power before and failed. It was probably why Odell was nothing, but a body for him to boss around. His spell was missing something. It was why he was summoning all those dark spirits and from the new madness in his eyes, I was sure of it. He had found it.

CHAPTER 20

We floated behind the high members. Byron still unconscious and battered, whilst I was gagged and powerless. Our ankles wrapped by one of Jaye's strings which he used to pull us along behind them. He kept whistling a happy tune on the way. I cursed over and over. Even if my voice had gone, I would still swear at them.

I could say that all that defiance was because I was courageous or angry, but the truth was, I was afraid. They were taking us to the dungeon. A place that haunted my nightmares. I had never been there. I never dared to know what the place the high members sent those who disobeyed them to rot looked like. Because deep down I knew I would end up there one way or another.

I saw the black door which was trimmed with a circle of yellow crystal beads. *Bubbles.* I didn't want to go in. I wriggled, trying to break my bonds somehow. My fear rising with each step, but when I was pulled inside the dungeon, alongside Byron, I was ... mesmerized by how beautiful and ominous it was.

The place was one big black room, with long illuminating torches that lit the moment we entered. Huge purple crystals dangled from golden chains across the ceiling, like icicles.

Purple, how fitting.

Pari raised his hand, palm down and from the ground rose a bladed black crystal. His hand brushed the surface and he whispered something. The blade glowed, as two purple crystals detached from their chains and floated down toward us. The side of the crystal opened to a hollow belly, wide enough for one person. I tried to wriggle free again, but the shadows tying my wrists tightened, cutting through the skin. I winced.

"Put them in," Pari ordered, and immediately Jaye twisted his wrist. His strings pushed me into a crystal and Byron into another one.

"Here's your new home, witchling. I hope you enjoy your time here," Jaye said before whistling, calling his strings back. Oh, hexing pixies, how much I wanted to rip him apart. The crystal sealed me in, but I could still hear his voice that said, *it will be short.*

I banged at the crystal with anger, frustration and despair, which filled me up. The ropes suddenly vanished from my body, making me slump back. The cord in my throat also loosened and I coughed, violently and repeatedly. By the time I managed to muster a roar, the high members had disappeared.

The crystal I was trapped in jolted as the chain pulled me up. Byron's crystal floated beside mine. The torches dimmed and died out, leaving the place with only the soft glow of the purple crystals.

"Byron!" I shouted, calling him. He was still unconscious, and I began to worry. He wasn't dead, I was sure of it. Pari wouldn't bother imprisoning him if he wasn't alive. But I didn't know the extent of his injuries. They could be fatal.

"Byron," I shouted again, this time with another bang. "Byron, for bubble's sake, wake up!"

I leaned closer to try and see if he was moving and I cried out when I saw his head moving. "Ah! Byron! Come on! Wake up!"

"Why are you screaming, dear Tia?" he said, his voice normal enough to know he only fainted. I hoped.

"Because I thought you were dead! How are you feeling?" I said, loudly.

"Like I've been celebrating in the tavern for two days," he said with a groan and to my dismay he reached for his head. I was hoping he wouldn't notice the ...

"Blood! Tia! I'm bleeding!" he said with a shrilling gasp. He tried to stand only to notice where he was. "What in the mountain happened?"

"Well ..." I gave him a quick summary of what he had missed in his brief coma.

"But, we were so close," Byron said staring at his bloodied hand.

"I know," I said, hugging my arm, before sliding down to sit on the hard surface. I barely fit. The world closed in on me. This was my fault. I should've known not to trust Rham.

They blocked my powers, and soon they will take my life. I was useless. No, I was worse than useless. If Pari managed to take my power with his spell, it would be disastrous. He was already a tyrant with fake stolen powers. Imagine if he had the endless pool of wielding powers! I shuddered at the darkness he would shed on the world with his shadows.

I was such an idiot for reacting so quickly when Jaye came to Paiza. Rhein was right. I should've trusted him. But I was afraid. I guessed even though I ran away and found a new home, the fear of this place always haunted me and locked my soul in an invisible prison. I was never truly free from them, and I was giving up on the possibility that I ever would.

A bang sounded from Byron's crystal. Then another, and a third thud. His anger echoed throughout the dungeon.

"Bubbles, Byron! Stop it," I called.

"No, we have to leave. We were so close. I was so close to seeing my Janie again," he said. I could see his dark silhouette banging on the glowing walls of his crystal. And for the first time I saw how this place took a toll on him.

"They are magical crystals. There is no way out!" I shouted at him.

"No, there is a way. There is always a way. I didn't come all this way to give up now. I didn't miss Janie this much for nothing. I had to lie, sneak around, smuggle gadgets, and con the poor callers here. Did you know one of them was lashed because of me? Did you even know they lashed the callers?"

No, I didn't.

"I did all of that and more to protect my city, to protect my family, to protect you. I am not giving up and neither should you."

The lack of fear in his voice and his utter conviction and belief in me snapped me out of my dark thoughts. He was right. I didn't run away and build a life, a very beautiful life, to give up right now. Bubbles, I kept giving up, and it was bubbling time for me to stop being so wrapped up in my own issues. I stood up, for me, for Byron, for the callers and more importantly, for Paiza.

I closed my eyes and reached deep inside of me. *Come on, stars, hear me out.* I felt a wall stifling the answering cries of my powers. I pushed deeper and deeper and I screamed as I cracked it open. I screamed as my powers erupted from me. My whole left side burned, but I didn't care.

I would burn and die before I allowed anyone to take my powers. No one could take them from me. *No-one.* My piercing screams continued as the promise of burning them all with me blazed through my soul. The crystal around me cracked and I dropped to the floor, with such force, I cracked the marble floor to pieces.

I looked up and shot my power at Byron's crystal, letting my magic wrap around him, which gracefully descended him from the crystal. I waved my hand before him, healing him from every injury. He touched his face, feeling his flawless skin andand to my surprise, he bowed.

"Thank you, dear protector."

"Now," I breathed through my pain. "Stay here. I have to go fight some magic thieves."

"Not alone, you are not," Rhein's voice echoed in the dungeon, and I whirled my aim toward the door. There he was, standing by the door with another man by his side. I pulled back my powers.

Burk and Rhein. *They're here.*

CHAPTER 21

"Rhein!" I ran to him. "You're here!" Our bodies collided as I threw my arms around his neck, and he picked me up in a tight embrace.

"Are you alright, Purple Hair?" Rhein whispered, burying his head in my hair.

"Yes, we're alright. We're alright." His hands dug deep into my back as he gripped me tighter. I didn't want to let go, either. The feel of him here, warm and strong, steadied me and filled me with hope.

"But how?" I asked stepping back and reaching my hand to Burk who took it and squeezed it. "How did you come here? And how did you know where we were?"

"The mountain transported us directly to you," Rhein said, his eyes wide with wonder as if he himself didn't believe the possibility of that statement. No wonder the members wanted the magic of the mountain, given how it broke through their wards so easily.

"But they'll know you're here."

"Your power is linked to the mountain and their powers are linked to yours. This would feel like one of them is performing a big spell," Burk said, "when they broke the machine, we had to take advantage of that spell and come and get you."

"Burk," I went and hugged him too, briefly. "My magic is broken, Burk." I said the words I wished I had said to him back in Paiza.

"Oh, no child," he said, taking my hand in his, shaking his head. "Your powers, the Magic of the Stars, which are not small, are linked to an ancient source of magic. This link disturbed both of your powers. You were pulling away from the mountain and the mountain was pulling you in. This is why the mudslide and all those natural incidents were happening. You didn't reach a balance," Burk said, as his hands moved in circles to draw the connection.

"What? How long did you know that?"

"After you told Rhein that your magic was broken, I figured it out. It's not broken, child. You're just not used to the connection, so your body called upon double the power you normally use and that's why its malfunctioning."

"Just like that? No," I said, not believing what he said. It was not that simple. "I came back for no reason? I risked all of you over nothing?" My head hurt. This was too much.

"No, child. It is never so simple. The high members would've found a way to get to you. They will always be a threat with their wielding magic."

"And they may discover us at any moment. We have to go."

"No, wait. They're not wielders," I said softly, as my mind was trying to understand this mountain connection and how my magic was not broken and this whole miserable journey back to the court would have been easily avoided if I just told Burk about my broken magic. *Wait.* I realized something.

"You didn't tell me the mountain was broken too!" I snapped at Burk. "I kept asking you about the mudslide and the other natural incidents. You both," I pointed at him and Rhein, "weren't honest with me too."

Rhein brushed his hair back, looking very sheepish, "Yes, we all have to communicate better from now on."

Burk ignored everything and asked, "What do you mean they're not wielders?"

That brought my focus back to the court and the fact that we were standing in the dungeon waiting for the members to come and kill me for my power, so finally, I was totally honest and told them everything. From the well to the high members absorbing raw powers and ended it with their intentions to steal my magic and become true wielders.

"This changes everything," Burk said, rubbing his chin. His eyes sharp and serious. "If we can take their source of power, we can easily defeat them."

"Exactly!"

"What are you talking about?" Byron asked, leaning closer.

"I have to destroy the well," I said with a clap.

"*We,*" Rhein corrected me, "*we* have to destroy the well and lucky for us, we came prepared," Rhein said, dropping a sack he had tied to his back.

He pulled out two copper disks and gave them to Byron. The metal expanded at his touch, covering his arm, shoulder and chest. A thin and elegant armor that I was sure wasn't easy to break materialized. I noticed Rhein was wearing a similar one.

"If Janie could see me now," Byron said flexing his arms. The purple light shimmered on the smooth surface like waves.

"And this," Rhein said pulling a copper blade, "if you aim at someone and press this button, it will charge a huge amount of electricity, enough to render the person unconscious."

Byron's eyes gleamed with excitement as he moved it closer to his face for examination, but Rhein cautioned him, pushing his hand and the copper blade away from Byron's face.

"And to you, my child," Burk pulled a smooth surfaced rock from his robe. A streak of shimmering rainbow danced across it. I raised my eyebrow at it, and he added, "It's a gift from the mountain, enchanted with a calling spell. It'll help you understand your connection better and anchor your magic."

"Thank you," I said, gratefully. I bit my lips, feeling the shame of not trusting him disperse over me.

"Now, child. Chin up," he said, his finger pushing my chin up. "And smile."

Ah, his contagious joy. Oh, how I missed that. I sniffed, smiled and held my head high. As long as we had hope, I'd continue smiling.

My hand reached for it and when the tip of my finger brushed its surface, something in me clicked. I gasped and took a step back. It was the same feeling I always got from the notebook, but this was more balanced. Binding and unbinding my powers, then linking myself to the mountain didn't break my own powers. I wasn't broken. *I wasn't broken.* Those thoughts rang in my soul.

What I was wrong about was keeping my struggles to myself.

"I brought more," Burk said pulling more pouches from his robe. He opened them and I was taken back by the number of rocks he had inside them.

"The mountain is stronger than those thieves."

"Great to have you here, cousin and Burk my magical man. I thank you both for the armor, but what is the plan?" Byron, who somehow had become the voice of reason in our group, said.

"First, we find the well," I said with a determined clap.

***

With careful stealth, we crept out of the dungeon and walked through the hallway. We met one caller on the way and before I got the chance to bewitch him to forget seeing us, Byron aimed his blade and stunned the poor man.

"Byron!" I hissed at him. "Be careful!"

"Sorry."

He squeaked and didn't resist when Rhein took the blade from him.

Stepping over the poor unconscious caller, we reached the end of the hall and somehow Rhein noticed the stiffness in me, and his hand reached for mine.

I took a breath and pointed at the wall, "Here, there's a hidden door."

"Do you know how to open it?" Rhein asked.

"No, Jaye just whistled," I said, my hand reaching to pull a lock of hair.

"Let the stone anchor you and open yourself to the magic," Burk said, sounding like the mentor he was and always would be.

I nodded.

I let go of Rhein's hand and pulled the rock from my pocket. I held it close to my heart and took a very deep breath before closing my eyes and releasing my powers. It cast a net across the wall, and my soul shined with the rush of power. The rush of focused pure magic. It felt like the broken pieces inside of me fell back to the right places.

I was myself again and I loved it.

"Focus," I heard Burk say.

I narrowed the projection of my powers into the place where I knew the door existed. The wall was nothing but cold lifeless stone, but then I felt it. A ripple of wrongness emanating from the middle.

"I feel it," I said almost in a whisper.

"Control it," Burk said.

I nudged the door, asking it to open, but something nasty resisted me. I nudged again and it again pushed back. I huffed with frustration and pushed harder, well more like burst through it, as the wall slashed open in a wider crack than what I saw Jaye summon.

"Not exactly controlling it, but good attempt," Burk said

"Well, it's wide enough for us to enter," Rhein winked at me before pulling out a stick that he used to shine a white light from, like a market lamp, before walking through the wider than intended slit in the wall. One by one, we followed him through the slit and down the narrow spiral staircase. His light guiding our way.

I shivered as we entered the damp cave and circled the well. I could feel the dark magic slithering underneath an ancient wooden lid.

"Lay the rocks around the rim," Burk said, giving each one of us a pouch.

I took my pouch and I reached inside to grab few pieces. A shiver ran through my body at the weight of their powers. The rocks weren't just part of the mountain's magic. They were part of its core, of its soul.

I sent a wave of respect and appreciation towards it. Piece after piece, we placed the rocks on the rim. The well shook. At first it was only a vibration, then the cave around us shook so hard, I had to clutch the well and was unable to prevent a few rocks from my pouch from falling on the floor.

"Is it working?" Byron asked, as he too was holding the well to be able to stand.

"No, we're not done yet; I haven't started the ritual." Burk said, as the worry on his face scared me.

"Is it resisting us then?" Rhein asked, pulling an unfamiliar cylinder-shaped object.

"No. It's not the well," Burk said. I could feel it too. Something else was tampering with the place. A magical pull.

A thunderous wail shook the well and I shut my eyes, as I fell, my knees burning from the impact. I grabbed the well rim and stood. I wanted to move but an invisible wall hit me.

"What just happened?" Byron said touching the air, feeling the wall.

"We're trapped," Rhein said, as our eyes met. *This was bad.*

Wind engulfed us, shaking our world. It felt like the well was being snatched out of its roots. *Hex!* I closed my eyes, held the well tightly and focused on not falling. A shadow eagle descended upon us before splitting into hundreds of eagles, as darkness fell upon us.

CHAPTER 22

Find the light.

I dug deep into my powers, squeezing the anchoring rock in my palm. With my powers coming to my aid, my skin radiated a purple light. I pushed further and the light blazed out of me, shining like a jeweled star and slashing through the shadows, lifting the darkness.

My hand gripped the well as I panted, still not used to this surge of power, before pulling myself up. Burk, Rhein and Byron were still there with me, standing, eyes wide with amazement at where we were. *The roof.* We were on the roof of the pentagon, right in the middle of the ritual alter, on top of my spot with the five carved stars.

Fire erupted inside the crystal poles, casting a blue hue over the place. Each member, including Odell, stood in front of their dedicated pole in their ceremonial robes. They were ready to cast their spell. They knew we were at the well.

"Time after time you tried to defy us, Daughter of the Stars, but we always rose higher and stronger," Pari snarled.

"Not this time," I whispered and growled at him. My magic felt my rage and sparks crackled out of my hands and eyes. *You have no claim on me.*

"You have lost," he rasped, spreading his arms wide. His robes slipped, revealing the new rune inked all of over his forearm, creating a foul pattern.

Before I could react, three shadow birds leapt at us. I covered my face and when I removed my arm, I saw each member holding one of my friends. Burk stood with Rham's staff under his chin. It was thrust so far into his throat, Burk was standing on his toes, trying not to choke. The spirit wielder didn't look me in the eyes. Byron was on his knees by Jaye's feet, his hands clasped over his ears and his eyes were wide with horror. *Rhein*. I looked around and found him in a bubble of water hovering before Cato, suffocating.

"No!" I called, "Don't you dare hurt them!"

I reached for my magic. Maybe if I was fast enough, the mountain could help me? I called for it, but sensing my need to fight, Pari raised his hand and my three friends screamed. I withdrew my power. Every light in me dimmed.

"Good star," Pari smiled, victorious, "let us begin."

The members spread their arms wide, their forearms covered with the same new ink stenciled onto Pari and they began to hum. An incantation in a language I had never heard. It was more like grunts than words.

I slammed my fists on the well. My heart bleeding. Rhein was drowning. Byron was going mad and Burk was on his last breath. I had doomed us all.

"Stop this!" I shouted. Tears piling in my eyes.

The humming continued. Flints of dark flames appeared on each members' chest. It floated down their body and ignited a fire on their feet. The fire blazed through lines connecting the pentagon and linking it to my spot.

Focus. Tia. Focus. I brought the stone to my chest. My whole body shook with panic and fear. *Oh, bubbles!*

"Please work. Please help me," I whispered as I brought the rock to my lips. It glowed and I could feel something rattle inside of me. I reached for it, wielding it to help me, to break me free.

"Hurry," I whispered to myself as the fire slithered around me in a circle.

The humming continued, rising and demanding more power.

I felt a tug inside of me. I hoped it was my magic fighting back, but no. I screamed, dropping the stone and clutching my heart as I felt something reach inside of me, trying to snatch my soul.

I gasped at the realization. They were calling me. They were calling my magic, my soul, my whole existence. The pain surged inside of me, as if the fire they wielded burned every vein in me. I cried out and curled up on the floor.

My limbs were being pulled apart. I was stretched to my limits. The pain rose from my lungs up to my throat bringing with it a heartbreaking wail. The magic inside of me, that purple light from the stars was being poisoned, twisted into something evil. My heart thumped so hard, it wanted to explode. To end it.

Death was coming. I could sense it. Death was coming for me, again.

You beat death once. A voice. A male voice I had never heard before echoed through the pain. *You can beat death again.*

"I beat death," I mouthed, inhaling sharply, sucking in the pain and forcing myself to open my eyes. My whole body was sweating and shaking, but I pushed through. I pushed with whatever little that was left in me, and I reached for the rock once more before placing it on my burning heart.

"I call on the mountain," I cried to the dark sky above me, as I laid on my back. "I call on the bond that ties our fate and existence together."

"I call on the mountain," I shouted, loud and true.

"We are your people and we call on you to save us. Help us fight back. Free us!"

My throat was dry, and I couldn't call anymore. Yet, right there, as I was on my back, almost dead, I heard it. The echo. The sound of the mountain reaching out to me, answering my call. The pentagon shook with a thunderous rumble. Gray clouds suddenly materialized above us, as a downpour of glittering rain fell, washing away every spell and flame the members had conjured.

I leaned on my elbow and breathed as the rain cooled my body and returned my magic to its original purpleness. I steadied my breath and looked around, trying to find Rhein. He was on the floor, completely soaked, but coughing water out of his lungs. He was on the floor, completely soaked, but coughing water out of his lungs. Good, he was alive! Rham's staff fell dead on the floor and whatever voice Jaye had used to torture Byron had stopped. The three of them stood free from the member who'd imprisoned them.

I balanced myself and dragged my feet until I managed to shakenly stand up with them. I whispered a *thank you* to the rock. The mountain answered our request. It helped us. But now, it was up to us to save ourselves. It was on us to end this.

I located Pari, leaning on his pole, and was for the first time ever, utterly disheveled. His face hollow with disbelief. He didn't think his spell would fail. Well, that ego and audacity lead to his demise.

"Pari!"

I shouted, feeling my soul fill with a decade worth of unexpressed rage.

"It's time for you to fall."

Light blazed out of me, hitting Pari and throwing him onto his back. I called for my magic from the mountain and hit Pari again, this time not stopping. His body was blasted off the roof.

Around me, small battles had begun.

"Your armor is a weapon, Byron."

Rhein's voice echoed across the roof, as he jumped, with a cloud of white steam thrusting him over Cato. His armor gleamed with energy. He slashed the old wielder with a sharp copper blade that manifested out of his palm.

Byron, who was dodging Jaye's strings, understood what Rhein meant and raised his arm as a string sought to slash him. The thin metal flared up like a shield and absorbed the string's magic.

"Ha! You thought using my Janie's voice would weaken me?! You thought using her would break me? Oh no, dear sir. She brings me life and I fight for her. I fight for her!" he yelled, and as if the mountain was fighting for their love too, the rain drops gathered around Jaye and choked him, taking his voice away.

How fitting.

Burk didn't have to do anything to Rham. The poor man was clutching his staff, scared and confused. Odell, however acted on his own for once and conjured a wooden stake which he aimed at Burk. I was about to hit him with my light, when Burk called the water around us, forming a long powerful whip. He slashed Odell, aiming to disarm him, but for some reason, Odell's presence departed, leaving behind a pile of white goo.

"What in the bubbles?" I said, looking at Burk.

"A homunculus," he said, blinking in disbelief. "He wasn't even human."

"What is real anymore?" I looked around, assessing the situation. Byron, euphoric with his victory, was circling Jaye's trapped body.

Rhein held a blade at the throat of a bleeding Cato. Burk stood between a frightened Rham and the goo that used to be Odell.

Was that it? Did we win?

But no, of course it wasn't that easy.

The shadow form of Pari shot out of the sky and down to the roof, crashing on top of the well. I immediately pushed my friends and Rham away behind the tree. *Protect them, my friend.* I stood, tentatively waiting to release all my magic, waiting to strike.

Pari panted deep and hard, his nostrils flaring with fury. He kneeled and smashed his hands into the broken well. Streaks of black pulsing magic appeared on his arms. He was absorbing the remaining magic out of the well.

"Waste of magic," he rasped as the streaks reached his neck and trickled up to his jaw and face.

"Weak. Pathetic. Undeserving. That power was meant for me."

"And what are you?" I said, steady and for once, sure of myself and my worth.

"All this time I thought I was a disappointment to you because I was what you said I was; broken and weak. But no; I now understand. You're disappointed because you were envious. *You* are the true weak one."

Pari only laughed and rose. The dark well's power danced around him.

"You have all this power, and you did nothing with it! If it wasn't for me, you wouldn't even know how to use it! I took this court by force and made it the feared authority that it is today. We are not all as privileged as you, to be born with magic, Daughter of the Stars. We take what we are owed. We take what life owes us."

"Life owes you nothing," I spat, falling to my knees, banging the marble with my fists. A wave of purple light, my purest and strongest light, rippled through the floor, cutting the marble toward Pari. It was meant to hit him, but this time he was prepared; this time he had the well.

His shadow of birds rose and shielded him from my light. I stood, ready to send another blaze, when his swarm of shadows melted together to form one giant serpent dragon that flew right at me. I conjured a ball of light, protecting me from the shadow, but the dragon was not affected. It circled the ball and lifted me off the roof, flying me up to the sky.

My heart sank to my stomach as I rose higher, the pentagon becoming a dot beneath me. *Bubbles and warts!* The dragon flew up, twisting and turning in a nauseating motion, as I gripped the rock tighter. *This was not how I die.* I closed my eyes and with a cry, I conjured flaming thorns around my ball and commanded it to move fast. Bit by bit, it slashed the dragon and I dived down between the clouds and cold night sky. I breathed in the air, calling the magic of nature around us to aid me; to give me its strength. Right before I crashed onto the roof, the wind answered me, easing my fall into a graceful float.

My feet touched the cold destroyed marble and with another cry I raised my hands, as the five crystal poles were yanked from the floor and crashed with all their magic and flames onto Pari. The impact boomed through the roof, pulsating across the sectors.

I had my magic. I had the mountain and now I had nature on my side. Pari was doomed. I walked toward him, waiting for him to rise from the rubble and try and attack me, but nothing came from him. *Was he dead?*

Suddenly, an eagle flew from between my feet and snatched the rock from my hand. I swayed, the balance between me and the mountain distorted. *No, no, no!* I tried to conjure my light only to have the pain in my arm return. It was sharp and paralyzing, but the pain of losing my anchor, of the impending loss scared me and hurt me more.

A blast exploded from the rubble of smashed crystals that had thrown me onto my back and before I could understand what happened, Pari was on top of me, pinning me down. The broken marble digging into my back.

"I will always rise higher," Pari's voice hissed in my ear. It felt as if a nail was grating my soul. His fingers dug into my chest and his shadows penetrated my heart; extracting my magic out of me. I choked and coughed; the taste of bitter iron filled my mouth. *Blood.* I was choking on my own blood.

"True, you are stronger," I said, blood dripping down my chin, "but if I fall, I am taking you with me." My finger drew a pentagram into the marble, and I opened my mouth and uttered the incantation from the black notebook. It would kill us all, but we were dying anyways. We could at least take these hexing members with us.

Pari looked confused at me and then somehow understood what the spell was about, as fear flickered in his eyes. *Good.* I continued mouthing the spell.

"Stop it," he said, taking his hand off my chest and clasping it on my mouth. Not fast enough, because I was done.

There was no booming or rumbling after that spell. No, it was soft and slow. An ancient magic awoke up from its eternal slumber. Pari feared it and stepped off me as a thread of soft purple light bloomed from my chest and gracefully drew a pentagram above me. I was in a trance.

My magic reached out. Reached so high up, higher than the clouds I visited a moment ago. I was among the stars. And there, among those glittering orbs, was one particular star. That star, the one I saw when I was back in Paiza, greeted me. It shone brightly and excitedly as my light reached it.

"Come," I mouthed. The star moved out of its orbit and the world shifted.

"Stop it." I heard an echo of a faraway soul. A panicked, no ... a scared soul, but I didn't care. I felt light and happy. I had finally found my connection to this star. A connection I never knew I craved. I wanted it to come. I wanted it to merge into me and end everything. The star was happy to have finally found me, too. It came full of joy and with promises of peace.

I waited for you, it said. *I have been waiting for you since you were born.*

"I'm here," I whispered.

Someone, the same scared soul, wrapped its hands around my neck, trying to choke me. He hummed spells, trying to cut my connection to my star.

We can't allow him. He is evil.

"No, he is lost," I said to the star, reaching for the soul's hand. "Be free."

My newfound light covered him and within two breaths, the soul was set on fire, releasing him from his misery.

Other voices reached me.

"What is happening?"

"Tia, child, break the spell."

"Purple Hair. Tia, love. Come back."

What are you talking about? I'm here.

"Come back to us. Whatever you're doing, stop it. We've won. Come back."

"Don't touch her."

It'll all be over soon, said the star and I closed my eyes, smiling. It was time.

From a distance, beyond the connection, a song was hummed. It was a calming melody that flew toward me. A song I'd heard many times before, during my school days, before the court. Back when I was an infant who hadn't learnt how to speak. It was a song that promised me the future.

You are not done, Datia, Daughter of the Stars, a voice told me, *this is not the end for you.*

The voice from my past snapped me awake. I jolted up, cutting ties to the star. The star's sadness crashed upon me. Its disappointment and longing. *I'm sorry.* I called for it. *I can't be with you now.*

I will wait for you, the star replied. Its voice drifting away. *I will wait.*

"Tia," Rhein said, and I turned.

"You're back."

His arms pulled me into a hug.

"I'm back. I'm here." I said. My heart was a flutter of excitement and disbelief. Through his embrace I noticed the destruction surrounding us, with broken marble and smashed crystals everywhere. Three members dead, one still scared to do anything, and one was, well, goo.

A thin white light appeared on the horizon, signaling the start of a new day and I held Rhein tighter. *We had done it. We have won. Bubbles!*

The melody, which I heard in my trance whistled through the wind. I turned, still in Rhein's arms, trying to locate the source and I could feel Rhein's fear that something wrong was going to happen from the way he pulled me closer.

"The tree," Byron said softly, "the tree is singing."

"And glowing," Burk added, as I turned toward the ever-blooming tree. It had defied the court through its existence alone. It was my only friend in this place. It sang and radiatied a green glow that throbbed. It was calling me.

I let go of Rhein, heading toward it.

"Tia!" he held my hand, urging me not to go.

I smiled.

"It's alright. It's a friend."

"Tia, darling, maybe you shouldn't." Byron said, taking a step toward me, but Burk stopped him.

"It's alright," I nodded at them. I reached the tree and extended my hand, resting my palm on it. The melody sang through me, healing my body and my soul.

The glow increased and drowned us all in nothing but green. Then, it decreased and with it, the tree started to disappear leaving nothing, but tiny green seeds floating around us and ... a man.

My hand was on his chest. I looked up and could see that his hair was green.

He smiled warmly before uttering two confusing words.

"Hello, daughter."

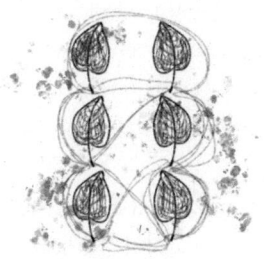

CHAPTER 23

What in the bubbles?

The tree had transformed into a man! He was a decade or so older than me and he wore nothing but brown pants. His hair, his short *green* hair, was flaked, by a few random leaves. He had the widest smile on his face, and *I felt I knew him.*

I took a step back, snatching my hand off this stranger, who actually looked exactly like...

"Odell?" I said, but the real Odell, or the fake one, or - *I didn't even know what to call that lump of goo* - didn't have green hair.

"Oh, how good it is to have lungs again," the green haired Odell said, closing his eyes and breathing deeply. His hands on his bare chest felt the expansion of his lungs.

"This place is a mess," green-haired Odell said, looking around.

"Excuse me, daughter. I should clean this first."

He passed me, his eyes narrowing with focus on all the destruction.

Daughter. Daughter. Why does he keep saying that?

"Emm, hello," I said following him.

"Yes," he replied not looking at me. He just raised his arm and green glowing leaves appeared around us, lifting and mending the broken marble and crystals which returned them to their original forms, as the ritual roof was perfectly restored within moments.

I was speechless.

I turned to Burk and pointed at Odell with my unspoken question of who this guy was, but Burk shrugged. He was more confused than I was.

"Ermm, tree man," I said stopping beside him, by the well.

He raised his hand to silence me, and I didn't argue as I saw how his smile turned to utter rage.

"This thing," he said. His voice was calmer than his eyes showed. He whispered a spell, raising a hand toward the well. A few veins from the walls' side glided across the marble across the marble and circled the well.

"Destroy it," the man said, as the veins obeyed. With a crack, they hardened their grip on the well, and with a snap, the well crumbled. The magic inside the well started swirling like a tornado and I took a step back, reaching for my powers, preparing for an attack, surprised that the well still had any power left. But the calmness of the green-haired Odell soothed me, and I trusted him as he took a step closer to it and flicked his wrist.

The tornado shot to the sky and dispersed into glittering sparks. The veins retreated to the wall, dragging the remnants of the well with them. Flowers blossomed around the pentagon and the dried dark vines turned a luscious green. The man kneeled on the ground, his palms pressed against the fresh marble floor.

"Thank you, mountain," he said talking to the water drops spilled on the floor. "Thank you for saving my daughter, my land and myself. We appreciate you."

The water glowed, before receding from the ground and vaporizing.

"Man of the magical tree," Rhein called as he stood by Burk and Byron. "Are you a foe or are you a friend? Are you a power abuser or are you a protector of the land?"

Green-haired Odell turned to face him. His wide smile returning.

"My name is Odell, Rhein, King of Paiza. I am the Wielder of Nature and a high member of the Court of Wizards; their only true wielder. Well," he turned to me, and placed a hand on my shoulder, "that was before my daughter Datia became a member too."

"What?" I said, pushing his hand away and walking to stand by the rest.

"Explain more," Rhein said, to which I would be forever grateful.

Bubbles. Why was my life this confusing?

"As you know by now, wielding magic had been a rare type of magic for few decades and so the court had a lot of powerful callers. We managed to support the lands and help those in need. But Pari always wanted more and during his travels he found this well. He started collecting magic from ancient objects and locations, then he moved to people. One by one, the other members followed him. When I found out about it and confronted him, he was too powerful and the well was packed with magic. I had the powers to destroy it and him, but I didn't realize he'd developed a spell to suck out a wielder's magic."

Odell is my father?

His eyes, though assertive, looked defeated. I recalled Jaye in the well cave saying something about Odell and a failed spell. A need to care for him overwhelmed me and I went by his side again. I rested my hand on his arm. He smiled at me, but I could see the sadness, the sense of failure. A look I knew.

"I couldn't stop the spell. I tried everything. And in order to prevent them from having my magic, I sealed myself inside the tree with a spell. You don't understand daughter, a wieldier's magic is so much more than what they showed you. I admit, I was afraid."

"I understand," I said. How could I not? I was about to destroy the whole court just so they wouldn't take my magic.

He looked at Rhein, "I am the protector of the land, King of Paiza. I was waiting for the day when someone would come and have the ability to stop them. Someone who was powerful and strong enough to tell them no, and that was *you*, daughter."

"Explain," I said softly, "the daughter part."

"Ah, well. Many moons ago. I had fallen in love with a beautiful woman. A farmer's daughter two cities away. She had brown hair, big black eyes and she was funny, courageous and somehow clumsy."

He laughed as his eyes filled with memories.

"We parted ways and I thought that story has ended, until you arrived at court. You, with your bright spirit and curly brown hair. I was a tree by then and I ached to know I couldn't protect you. I tried my best to support you, but you found your way. You did what I couldn't do."

I hesitated to believe him. How was this possible?

"Feel it yourself," he said, sensing my questions. He opened his energy to me, I stood straight and closed my eyes. I reached for my powers, letting it seep through us. The moment our powers merge, I believed. I believed with all my heart. The familiarity, the connection was true. It was like his powers were a part of mine and I was a part of his. *He was my father.*

Beautiful shining hope filled my soul with light. I had always discarded the idea of family, thinking they had deserted me, but here I was, stood at the start of a new era with my new family and the one I never knew existed.

I stepped closer and hugged him. He did not expect that.

"I heard you," I said.

It was he who told me I won over death. It was he who pushed me to be better.

"I heard your songs," I added, as I felt his arm around me.

"I'm sorry I missed your transformation," he said.

I pulled back, eyeing him with a question.

"The hair. I had black hair though, but we have a special trait in our family. Our hair changes color when our powers mature," he said touching my purple locks.

"It's not an accident?" I said, gawking at him.

"No. It is your birth right," he smiled.

From the moment that color changed, I thought it represented my brokenness. Even though I loved it, I labelled it as a sign of my survival. Now, I realized, it was more than that. It represented my heritage, my family, my true powers. And I loved it even more.

"What now?" Byron called, killing an emotional moment as always.

"Now, I try to repair all the damage the old members inflicted. It will take years for the land to recover. I have to restore the faith in wielders again. With your powers and mine, daughter, we can do it."

"Tia," Rhein called, holding out his hand for me, "may we speak?"

I nodded and took his hand, leaving my father and the rest behind us. We stood by the edge, close to the wall of greenery in our tattered clothes, covered in dust and soot. Two survivors of yet another magic battle. A breeze danced around us, making my locks bounce around me.

"I need to stay," I blurted out before Rhein could say anything.

"He's my father and I do want to fix what those idiots did. Rham also needs me. They took him to the brink of death and I know you won't agree with that, but he is a kind, but lost soul. Plus, I can now learn more about my magic and I will always have my connection to the mountain. I will transport to you, every now and then. I'm still Paiza's protector and I do want to live there, just not yet."

"I know," he said, as a crooked smile formed which slowly disorientated his scars. He pulled a watch from his pocket and gave it to me. The jitters in my stomach were back. I missed this feeling. *Bubbles, I missed him.*

"I made this for you."

He placed it in my hand. It was a beautiful piece of silver etched with stars and gears that intertwined to form one big star. The numbers and the watch hand were colored purple and circled by a copper rim.

"It's beautiful," I chirped, tying it around my neck like a necklace before saying, "your hand please."

He gave it to me and I shivered at his touch. I whispered something and kissed the inside of his wrist. I could feel him shiver too, under my kiss.

I pulled back revealing a small black star tattoo.

"I have a part of you. You should have a part of me, too. This time, willingly given."

"You will always belong with me and I you," Rhein whispered leaning closer, his forehead resting on mine, our noses touching.

"I love you."

"I love you way more," I said giggling.

"We need new members," Odell said loudly, interrupting our moment, even though he was speaking to Burk.

"I can sense great powers and a sense of reliability from you."

"We will not let you steal our magical man too," Byron said jumping before Burk.

Burk tapped Byron on the shoulder and said, "Don't worry, Lord Byron. I will never leave Paiza. Thank you for your offer, high member, but I have my own city to take care of, as well."

"The court will owe the people of Paiza forever."

"Just leave us be and we'll be fine," Rhein said offering his hand. Odell shook it.

"I can help you go home, if you like," Odell said and they all nodded.

I cuddled Rhein whispering, "I'll see you soon," then hugged Burk.

"I'm always here for you, child," he assured me.

"Darling Tia. I shall miss you terribly," Byron said as he embraced me.

"I'll come visit more often than you think," I said giggling. "Don't forget, we have Anna's wedding!"

"Will you tell Janie how heroic I was and how much I suffered?"

"Of course. Without you, nothing was possible."

"Marvelous."

I hugged him again and then stood by Odell, my father.

I waved at them, and with a clap Odell transported them back to Paiza.

I touched the watch on my chest. This wasn't goodbye. This was the start of my new life.

THE END

ACKNOWLEDGMENT

"She remembered who she was and the game changed."

- Lalah Delia

Thank you, Reader for reaching the end and thank you for waiting for this part's release. I've got to admit, writing this book during a global pandemic was not easy, but as always, Tia's story has guided me back to the light.

I dedicate this book to my amazing bestie, Abeer Al-Kubaisi. As soon as I told her about Tia's story prior to writing it, she became my pillar of support and encouraged me to develop the story, further. I had planned for the story to only be one part, but her motivation and support encouraged me to develop the concept of the Court of Wizards and delve further into Tia's life, both within the Court and beyond. For that, I have written this part to provide a glimpse into the powerful magic of that Court and offer an idea into how power is capable of corrupting a soul in so many different ways.

I also wanted to explore the situation where an abused victim is coercively dragged back to their abusers. My heart bled as I wrote those scenes, but I had to believe in Tia, in the same way that I believe in every human out there who is suffering and hoping that they can overcome their tragedy and find their true voice and their true homes.

I would like to thank my publishers at Hamad bin Khalifa University Press for believing in me and in Tia. Their guidance and patience helped me find my voice again. A big thank you goes to my development editor, Robert Eversmann, who has been alongside me from the beginning and helped me bring Paiza, its people and its gadgets to life. Robert also played a huge role in helping me navigate Tia's relationship with the high members. I would like to also thank my other editor, Zeid Kabbara, who helped add an element of suspense to the second part of Tia's journey.

Dear Reader, I really hope that you have enjoyed Tia's adventures and that she has somehow brought you a touch of magic and helped enhance the belief that adversary is never permanent, no matter how difficult you may feel your predicament is.

Kummam